DATE DUE

MAY 1 0 2013	MAY 8 2014
MAY 2 1 2013	JUN 0 3 2014
	SEP 2 9 2014
SEP 2 3 2013	NOV 1 9 2014
	DEC 1 2 2014
NOV 5 2013	FEB 0 3 2015
DEC 4 2013	APR 2 3 2015
DEC 1 6 2013	MAY 7 1 2016
JAN 6 2014	FEB 0 6 2017
FEB 6 2014	MAR 0 2 2017
FEB 1 8 2014	
APR 0 3 2014	
OCT 0 9 2014	

DEMCO 38-296

crazy beautiful

crazy beautiful

LAUREN BARATZ-LOGSTED

Houghton Mifflin

Houghton Mifflin Harcourt
Boston New York 2009

Houghton Mifflin is an imprint of
Houghton Mifflin Harcourt Publishing Company.

www.hmhbooks.com

The text of this book is set in Hoefler Text.
Book design by Carol Chu.

Library of Congress Cataloging-in-Publication Data

Baratz-Logsted, Lauren.
Crazy beautiful / by Lauren Baratz-Logsted.
p. cm.
Summary: In this contemporary retelling of "Beauty & the Beast," a
teenaged boy whose hands were amputated in an explosion and a
gorgeous girl whose mother has recently died form an instant connection when they meet on their first day as new students.
ISBN 978-0-547-22307-0
[1. Amputees—Fiction. 2. People with disabilities—Fiction. 3. Bullying—Fiction. 4. High schools—Fiction. 5. Schools—Fiction.] I. Title.
PZ7.B22966Cr 2009
[Fic]—dc22   2008040463

Manufactured in the United States of America
MP   10 9 8 7 6 5 4 3 2 1

DEDICATION

For Andrea Schicke Hirsch,
my dear friend since 1987

ACKNOWLEDGMENTS

Every book has its own cast of characters, as well
as another cast of characters who have helped along the way,
and this book is no different. Sincerest thanks go to . . .

Pamela Harty — *with whom I just got off the phone, for being my agent and*
friend

Everyone at the Knight Agency — *for all that you do*

Julia Richardson — *whom I just emailed, for being my editor and friend*

Everyone at Houghton Mifflin Harcourt — *for everything you do for my books*

The Friday Night Writing Group: Lauren Catherine, a.k.a. L2; Andrea
Schicke Hirsch; Greg Logsted; Rob Mayette; Krissi Petersen — *for your*
input and for being my friends

Lucille Baratz — *for keeping copies of my books in her purse to show doctors,*
waitresses, bank tellers, and random strangers, and for being my mom

Greg Logsted — *for being a great writer, friend, and husband, and for putting up*
with me

Jackie Logsted — *for making every moment of my life happier*

Finally, thank you to all the bloggers, booksellers, and reviewers
who showed early enthusiasm for this book, and to the readers who
will read it. *No writer is anything without people like you.*

crazy beautiful

LUCIUS

My arm rises toward my face and the pincer touch of cold steel rubs against my jaw.

I chose hooks because they were cheaper.

I chose hooks because I wouldn't outgrow them so quickly.

I chose hooks so that everyone would know I was different, so I would scare even myself.

"Lucius!" I hear Mom call from the bottom of the staircase. "If you don't hurry, you'll miss the bus. You'll be late for your first day!"

She sounds so excited.

Like I'm in a hurry to start sophomore year at a brand-new school. Like I'm in a hurry to be the new kid, especially looking like I do, when everyone else in my class will have already established themselves, their friendships and their cliques, back in freshman year. Like this will be something good, like it'll be anything other than the pure awful I know it will be.

Time to get dressed.

My room is like a white-walled cell. Oh, sure, it has the basics — bed, dresser, desk — but none of the frills my old room had. I have no CD player, no DVD player. I'm not allowed to have a computer, and I'm sure not allowed to have any science stuff anymore. Even the walls are bare.

I lost everything in the explosion — my father would say *we* lost everything — so a lot of what I don't have is punishment for that. Also, because we can't afford to replace a lot of things. Also, self-punishment. We could of course afford at least a few posters, but I don't want them. I want to be reminded all the time. I know the world won't let me forget, so I can't let myself forget either.

The dresser at least contains some decent new clothes, but the jeans I pull out are stiff with their newness, the long-sleeved black T-shirt I pull out stiff as well; I always wear long sleeves, even on the hottest days of summer, to cover my synthetic arms, which extend from just above where my elbows should be to my "wrists," where my hooks begin. When I pull on my socks, I think about how when I was younger I loved the feel of new socks against my skin: not faded or stained, never been washed or worn. But now everything feels *too* new, like I'm being forced into a costume for a play I want no part of. At least my sneakers, which I've been breaking in all summer, have the feel of something I know. It took me two weeks of solid practice to learn how to tie my own laces again, but I refused to get Velcro, and once I mastered those tricky laces, it was like everything else fell into place. In the beginning, I couldn't even pull on my own underwear without scraping my skin with the hooks, but now I can do it all, and do it fast; briefs instead of boxers, just in case anyone's curious. Some minutes, it's possible to forget how much has changed. And in my dreams, I always have real hands.

Down in the kitchen, Dad is in his usual spot (hiding behind the newspaper), Mom is in her usual spot (doing something at the counter), and my younger sister, Misty, is in her usual spot (being a pain wherever she is). Some days, I think Misty is okay, but mostly it's like she got the memo that kid sisters are supposed to be incredibly annoying and she follows those instructions religiously.

Misty is a smaller version of Mom — tiny, cute, and blond — while everyone has always said I favor Dad. Seeing as Dad is balding and paunchy, I always hope people understand when I say I just don't see it. But maybe they just mean the eyes are the same. Or maybe the nose. It's amazing how people can take just one small part of a person and draw massive conclusions.

"Pancakes, Lucius?" Mom offers, her back to me as she does some stuff in front of the microwave.

"No," I say, taking my seat at the kitchen table, "I'm good."

The cushion of the seat feels funny beneath my butt. It's as though the cushion of the seat at the table in our old kitchen, in our old house, knew my butt perfectly, but this cushion doesn't know my butt at all. It's the same as with the jeans and T-shirt, I guess: I don't know any of it, and none of it knows me.

I suppose it's not surprising.

The old house, we lived in it all our lives, all my life and Misty's, at least. This place? We've only been here a few months.

How long, I wonder, does it take a thing or a place or even a person to feel like home?

Mom puts a glass of orange juice on the table in front of me, fresh from the carton, even though I didn't ask for any. Dad still hasn't said a word. Misty, even though she's only twelve to my fifteen, is spending all her time checking out her own reflection in a handheld mirror. I think girls call them compacts. Or maybe only moms call them that. Or maybe only my mom. I wonder sometimes: Every time Misty looks in that mirror, is she expecting her reflection to have changed from the last time she looked? Who is it she's hoping to see? I could tell her, if I thought she'd hear me, that the thing about herself she wants to see change the most probably never will. The universe knows that's the case with me. I am an expert on that.

In the beginning, I used to look at myself in the mirror all the time, repulsed at what I saw, trying to surprise my own new image by jumping out at the mirror from the sides. What I saw never changed. Now I know it never will. I look like what I look like and except for getting gray and wrinkled will look like this for the rest of my life. It's not like I'm ever going to be able to do something simple, like diet or pluck my eyebrows — two of Misty's favorite activities — to ever change the way I look. It's not like I'm a starfish, able to generate new limbs.

And yet I accept what I've done, what I've become. I accept who I am, and what my future will undoubtedly be.

Mom must notice that I don't touch my juice, because she says, "You're not even going to drink anything, Lucius? Are you that nervous about your first day?"

"No," I say. "I'm not nervous at all." And I'm not — nervous, that is. It's pointless to be nervous when you know what the outcome of a thing will be. Nervous is only for when you *don't* know. "If I pull this switch, what will happen?" "Will the doctor tell me I won't make it?" "What will adding this one little chemical do to the potion?" "Does the pilot really know how to fly this plane?" No, I'm not nervous. I'm just not exactly looking forward to any of this. "I'm just not hungry," I tell my mom. "Or thirsty. That's all."

"Well," Misty says, "isn't anyone going to ask *me* if *I'm* nervous?"

"Of course," Mom says. "Are you?"

"*No,*" Misty says, with even more arrogance than I had at her age. Then her expression changes, as if she can't stop herself from feeling whatever she's feeling. "Well, maybe."

"You'll be fine," Mom soothes. "Just be yourself, and I'm sure everyone will like you."

It's such a Mom thing to say. If everyone in the world would just be themselves, then everyone else in the world would like them. As if it's ever that easy. If this were a year ago and Misty was angsting about starting something new, I'd tease her. I'd say, "Of course no one will like you, *especially* if you 'just be yourself.'" I'd say it because just like Misty got the memo that she's supposed to be a brat to me, I got the memo saying that as the big brother I am to make her life miserable. But I can't do that to Misty today. I know how much I've cost her already.

Of which she wastes no time reminding me, as she leans across the table after Mom pokes her head into the fridge, and hiss-whispers, "This is all *your* fault. If it weren't for you, we'd never have had to move in the first place."

Mom's head is still in the fridge and Dad's head is still behind his newspaper, so I don't think for more than a split second before raising one of my hooks and holding it over Misty's head. It's a menacing way to hold the hook. I know this. I've had too much practice this past summer.

I watch as Misty recoils from me, her brother, in horror, as I knew she would. It's its own brand of scary, seeing someone you're related to look at you with such fear in her eyes. It's a look I've seen before.

But I don't care, in the moment. In the moment, I just want to stop being reminded, if only just for a second. I want to take a break from being told that everything in our lives, all the millions of little changes, is my fault. It's all because of me me me.

Before Mom gets her head back out of the fridge, before Dad peeks over the top of the newspaper, I take my menacing hook and place it back on the table.

I try to smile at Misty, really smile — *It was all just a joke,* my smile says, begs her to believe, *you know?* — but she's not having any.

She doesn't trust me, and I can't really say that I blame her. Misty may be an annoying little sister, but she's not stupid.

So I try to pretend nothing out of the ordinary just happened. I reach for my juice glass with both hooks, but instead of using the hooks I use the plastic wrists of my prosthetics to grasp the glass and raise it to my lips. This is how I drink sometimes. I'm adept with the hooks for fine motor stuff — meaning grabbing or holding on to small objects — but for something like a glass I sometimes resort to this. The doctors told me that later I'd get used to holding on to bigger objects, but that in the beginning mastering the pincer grip would be enough, and that it would all come in time. But first, baby steps. And sometimes I regress. Better to regress than digress, I always tell myself.

I go to put the glass back down on the table, but something goes wrong. I make a misjudgment in spatial relations. Maybe it's because the glasses in this house are different from the ones in our old house. Maybe it's because the table is different. Maybe it's because I really am, no matter what I say, nervous; nervous about starting over in a new place. Whatever the cause, I misjudge, put the glass down too abruptly or too harshly, and can only watch as it totters, in that excruciating slow-motion way of forthcoming disaster, and then tumbles, sprawling a tiny sea of orange in the direction of Dad's beloved sports pages.

That finally gets his attention.

Gee, if I'd known spilling my orange juice was this effective, I'd have spilled it in Dad's direction every day when I was younger. Then maybe he'd have made time to do things with me like, I don't know, play catch in the yard. Not that I'm complaining or playing the neglected child card. I'll never do that. I know what I've done. I know who's responsible for everything in my life, past, present, and future. Still, a little catch would have been fun, when I still had hands.

Dad does a little jump in his seat, but maybe the cushions of these chairs still don't feel right to his butt either, because his reaction time and reflexes are off, and he can't save the Mets' scores from being drenched.

This can't be good. He always reads the paper in a particular order: front page first, because he says it's irresponsible not to; followed by sports; followed by whatever else he has time for. He won't like reading a soggy sports section.

You'd think a guy who likes reading the sports pages so much would have found time to play ball with his own kid.

But now I really do digress, and with good reason.

I'm sure he's going to yell.

All I wanted was a moment, just a second in which I could take a break from being reminded.

But Dad doesn't yell.

There have been times, many times before today, when I've wished he would.

He folds the sports section up in a ball and tosses it to the middle of the table, away from him. It's a good toss; there's something athletic about it. Then he snaps the front section as if he's opening it for the first time that day, as if nothing has happened.

I let out a breath I didn't even know I was holding.

That's when Dad peers at me over the top of his newspaper and issues one of his trademarked glares.

"Whatever you do today," he says, "don't louse it up. This is your last chance."

AURORA

I hear the dog alarm go off in the same instant I become aware of the first morning light in my room. I like rising early, like sleeping with the blinds open, because I'm scared of the dark.

In the dark, almost anything can happen.

The dog alarm isn't an alarm warning that there are dogs in the area or anything like that, and it's not a real dog sounding an alarm that there are burglars in the house. The dog alarm is a fairly large stuffed animal, light tan with white accents, its fur matted with the passage of years. In its belly is an alarm clock. When I first got it, when I entered grade school nine years ago, I could never wake up when it went off. Which is amazing, because the thing is really loud. You know: "Yip-yip-yip-yip-yip"? That's what it's like, like the fake dog is so excited that he might pee on the rug any second, and it doesn't stop yipping until you turn it off. There's no snooze button with the dog alarm. It is all-out sound or nothing. You are either sleeping in spite of it or you are awake.

My parents always used to say that it was astonishing how deeply I slept, that as a baby I used to terrify them because whenever they'd come to change my diaper in the middle of the night, I wouldn't even wake when they lifted my legs high up to remove the dirty diaper, wipe my privates, and slide a clean diaper into place. They said it was scary because it was like — and these words they hated to say out loud — it was like trying to diaper a dead baby. So when I got the dog alarm in first grade and I still couldn't be wakened easily, my mom would have to come in and turn it off before it drove her crazy, and then with me still with my eyes closed, she'd get me dressed for the day and then she'd guide me to the bathroom, gently pushing me, my eyes still closed, so she could brush my teeth. By the time I sat down to breakfast, I'd be raring to go — my mom always said I was the sunniest kid in the world once I was awake — and it would be like I'd never been asleep at all.

I know I should get rid of the dog alarm and get something cooler, something more suitable to my age. But I don't even know what that would be. My friend where we used to live, Gracie, had a Hannah Montana alarm clock, but I don't even know if that's something a kid my age would have anymore. What would girls our age have now? A Lindsay Lohan clock? No. Probably not. Maybe, I think sometimes, I should just get something in basic black? But my mom gave me that alarm and I can't stand to part with it. Now whenever the dog alarm goes off, I'm awake in the same instant. I'm no longer a heavy sleeper, having learned the opposite practice all the years my mom was sick.

I hug the dog alarm, whose name is Bowser, to my chest, thinking of the day ahead, dreading it.

Change has never been my favorite thing, maybe because so many of the changes in my life have been bad ones.

My dad, knowing this about me, has tried to keep things from changing too much for me too quickly. That's why, even though this is a new house, a new bedroom, he was careful to recreate as much of the old bedroom in the old house as possible. My dad is like that. If there were an award for being the best dad who ever lived, my dad would win it. His recreating my old room means that all my old furniture is here: the white bed with the fairy canopy, the matching dresser on which he used leftover paper from the Cinderella border to decorate the drawers, the sheer white curtains that love to dance in the breeze. I do realize that the fairy canopy and Cinderella accents, like the dog alarm, are too young for me now, but I like familiar things, my brief flirtation with Lindsay Lohan and basic black clocks notwithstanding. And it's been my experience that so long as I have all the hottest CDs, DVDs, clothes, and other things, no one ever seems to notice the rest. My dad also insisted I take this room, even though it's the biggest and would likely be called the master bedroom, because he knows I prefer the morning sun to the dying sun at the end of the day, and this is the one bedroom in the new house that greets the dawn.

The only other thing my dad insisted on — he really doesn't usually insist on much — was that we move here in the first place. He said the old house had become a mausoleum, and, despite my loud objections, he decided that wasn't healthy for either of us.

I let go of Bowser and roll out of bed, feel the coolness of the hardwood floors beneath my feet. It's odd. You'd think softer would be better than harder, right? And yet there's something comfortingly solid about this hardness beneath my naked toes, how it doesn't give to my weight at all, that it remains firm beneath my feet. It almost makes me temporarily believe the illusion that this new world could be a safer, steadier place. In our old house, it was all wall-to-wall carpeting in the hallways.

Some changes, I think, are good.

Once in the bathroom, I take a long shower, and when I come out I brush my hair one hundred strokes, just like my mom always taught me to, before styling it into something that the kids in my new school will hopefully take as familiar but special.

It's easy to pick out my first-day clothes, since I set them out the night before. My mom and I picked them out from a catalog earlier in the year, because she could no longer make it out to the stores, something she once upon a time loved so much to do. She used to say that her own mom, born in the Depression, hated to take her shopping, would just buy the quickest and cheapest things, and not much of that. Not that my mom was reckless with money, but she used to say she loved shopping for me, loved having the money to spend on buying me the kinds of things she would have loved to have for herself if she were growing up now. Hell, sometimes I'd have to tell her, "No! I don't need three different-colored versions of the same shirt. That style will go out before I even have the chance to wear them all. Put two of those back!"

That was one of the last things we ever did together, shopping from that catalog. She made sure I had the latest jeans, the latest top, the latest shoes, but nothing too flashy or unusual — again, familiar but special.

People at my old school, friends, sometimes said they thought I seemed too effortless, that I didn't bother trying to stand out or wearing makeup, like I didn't care whether people liked me or not. But of course I care. It's hard to be a human being and not care if you're liked. Or maybe it's not so much that I care about being liked as that I'd prefer, if given the choice, not to ever be hated by one and all. My mom always said a person needs only one good friend in this world, and it used to make me sad when she'd say that some people don't even have that.

At least back where we used to live I had Gracie. And I had a lot of other people, friends, as well.

As I'm dressing, the smell of pancakes drifting up the stairs is so strong that I hurry up and finish putting on my shirt, buttoning up my jeans. Then, as I follow the aroma down the stairs, I feel as though I'm following one of those smoky trails you'd see in a cartoon, the kind that are supposed to symbolize a really good smell.

When I get down to the kitchen, there's my dad, slaving over a hot griddle, wearing one of Mom's old frilly full-length aprons to protect his crisp white shirt and navy and crimson striped tie.

Sometimes I think my dad has it even worse than I do since Mom died. I had her for only fifteen years, five of which she was sick and then sicker until she was no more — cancer can take so much out of a person, until there's nothing left but a shell — while she'd been his best friend since they were my age.

I know that whenever he looks at me, he can't help but be reminded of her. I've seen pictures of her when she was the same age I am now, and though the hairstyles and fashions are different, when you line the pictures up side by side it's the same face repeated, the same eyes, the same dark color hair, the same smile.

As for my dad, he's a tall, burly guy, still young to be mostly bald but doing it all the same, with just a little bit of blond left around the edges, blue eyes behind steel glasses. My mom's frilly apron looks frankly ridiculous on him whenever he wears it, but I'm careful not to tell him this or even smile about it, because I know how hard he's trying, trying all the time.

"Can you pour the juice, princess?" my dad asks, using a spatula to flip the pancakes from the griddle to a china plate. The plate is white with gold trim: a thin stripe of gold inside and then a wide band of it circling the rim. My dad can't seem to get the hang of things, that the china is supposed to be for when company comes, while there's everyday dishes for when it's just us.

On the table, next to a crystal vase with fresh-cut flowers in it — lush peonies that he bought special from the florist, Mom's favorite flower — is a glass pitcher of hand-squeezed orange juice. I fill glasses for each of us as my dad sets our plates down on the table.

"Big day ahead, for both of us," he says, forcing a bright smile as he takes his seat, draping a heavy linen napkin in his lap. Using the linen means the laundry piles up more quickly, but I never tell him it'd be easier to just use paper, throwing it away afterward like the rest of the world does.

"Yeah," I say, forcing an equally bright smile, and lying through my teeth when I add, "but we're up for it."

"That's the spirit!" he says, drizzling maple syrup over his pancakes. He pauses, forkful of pancake in hand. "You're not nervous, princess, are you?"

"Of course not!" I lie again, punctuating my words with a cheery laugh for good measure.

"That's great," he says, content to eat at last, "just great."

I hope he doesn't notice that I'm just sitting there, that I'm not eating at all because my stomach is churning so badly with nerves.

He's almost done with his breakfast when I say, "Daddy?"

"What is it?"

"I was just wondering." I stop, unsure of how to proceed so he won't see how I really feel. "I was wondering," I go on, "if maybe we should drive into school together? You know, just this once? I thought, I don't know, maybe it would be fun. We've never done it before."

My dad is a librarian by profession, a school librarian, which is a good job for him since he loves books; we both do. My mom used to tell me that even when I was an infant, my dad would lie next to me on the floor, extending his arms high and holding a book over our heads as he read to me and I squealed, kicking my baby legs at the sound of his voice and the sight of all those pictures. But he's never been librarian at any of the schools I've gone to in the past.

Now things are different.

Back where we used to live, some of my friends had parents who were teachers at the same school, and those friends always hated it. And the friends who didn't have teacher parents? They all said they'd hate it if they were those teachers' kids too.

But I'm glad my dad and I will be in the same school now. It makes me feel safer somehow, for both of us. I think sometimes now that he needs me to look out for him just as much as, if not more than, I need him to look out for me.

"Oh, princess." It's like his whole cheerful expression collapses as he says this, and I swear I see tears forming in his eyes. "You're just worried about your old man, aren't you?" He reaches out a hand, pats the back of one of mine. "Well, don't be. I'll be fine, and more important, *you'll* be fine." He straightens up in his chair, as though steeling his resolve. "But I think it's important you start your first day out just like all the other kids. You belong on that bus with everyone else. Don't let feeling sorry for your old man get in the way of your good times."

I want to tell him, *wish* I could tell him, that he's got it all wrong: that in this moment, *just* this moment, I'm more worried about myself than I am about him, that I'm terrified of getting on that bus with all those people I don't know, everything new, everything different.

But I can't tell him that.

So instead, I just get my things together, give him a hug goodbye, and head on out the door to wait for the bus.

LUCIUS

It's not hard for me to decide where to sit on the bus.

If this were my old school, I'd sit all the way in the back. But even though the back of this bus isn't completely filled yet, I don't go there. Once I'm in school, once I'm in classes, the back row will be the place for me. I can hide out there. But not here. The back of the bus is where all the cool kids hang out, and I am not a cool kid, certainly not here, not yet, maybe never.

The middle of the bus?

Too many jock types and preppy-looking girls. First day of school, not even at school yet, and already it's possible to see where everyone fits in to the hierarchy. If there is a greater scheme of things, I am at rock bottom on that scheme. If I try to sit there, with the jock types and the preppy-looking girls, I know I'll get cold-shouldered or, worse, abused. I expect to get abused today — I'm not an idiot — but it's a little early in the day for that. I'm hoping to delay it until after lunch, at least. My reasoning? Do I need any?

So I take what is the perfect seat for me, the one that no one will ever object to my taking: the one right behind the bus driver. No kid in his right mind ever wants that seat. From now on, it'll be mine. Ownership, as they say, has its privileges.

I settle down lengthwise in the bench seat as the bus pulls away from the curb, meaning I place my back against the side of the bus, head resting against the grimy window, legs sprawled out across the bench so that any riders who enter after me — should they truly be losers enough to also want to sit behind the driver — will get the message and go sit somewhere else. From this vantage point, if I turn to my left, I have a view of the bus driver's stringy red hair. I'm thinking she might maybe want to wash it sometime this century. Swivel to the right, and I can check out the other kids, some of whom will no doubt wind up sharing some classes with me. I can't wait. Can they?

I can't say it looks like a particularly distinguished group. Oh, there's nothing wrong with any of them — at least not that I can see now, not yet — but they don't really look any different from kids in my old school. They're just your basic kids. Some may be nice. A few will be cruel. They'll worry more about what other people think than what they themselves think. There's really only one that bothers me from the start. That guy there — the one halfway between the middle of the bus and the back, long legs sprawling into the aisle so everyone who walks past either has to say "Excuse me" or try to step over those legs. He's got short, spiky hair so perfectly streaked in shades from brown to white-gold, you can almost see him sneaking trips to his mommy's salon to get it dyed just perfect. I don't like his shell necklace either, and I really don't like it when I hear him say to the girl sitting next to him, the girl with the red hair gathered into a ponytail, "Hey, did you get a load of the new crip sitting behind the bus driver?" I hear her giggle a response and I realize maybe I don't like her so much either.

Right around now, I am wishing I could have stayed at my old school.

But by the end of the last school year, my dad said it was no longer an option.

He said it was bad enough, the damage to our home. He said it was bad enough, what I'd done to myself. But now everyone was talking like I was crazy — even people who used to maybe be my friends were saying they thought that maybe I just might be dangerous — and he said enough was enough.

We would move to a new town, but not too far, so he wouldn't have to change his work. And I would be given one last chance: to prove I could live among civilized people. He didn't have to spell out the implied "or else." We all knew what he meant: or else I'd be sent away to some place where I couldn't be a danger to other people if not myself.

Now that Shell-Necklace Boy has used the word "crip," there is no longer any point in my checking out the other kids. Now that he has used the word "crip," he has opened the door for them all to talk about me, the boy who got on the bus with hooks for hands. The way he uses the word makes it sound as though I've somehow offended him personally and with great deliberation. And, oh, how they talk about me — as though I am also deaf and cannot hear them.

"I think I read about that dude in the city newspaper," I hear a different male voice say, not Shell-Necklace Boy. *Yeah?* I'm thinking. *You really expect anybody to believe you read the newspaper?* I tune them out. Instead, I study the back of the bus driver's hair again. She really should think about washing that hair someday. I really need to stop obsessing about her hair.

The bus slows for another stop.

I think to keep my eyes focused away from the person entering. If I don't make eye contact with other people, I can't see them looking at me with cruelty.

But something compels my gaze.

Entering the bus now is perfection. And it's not just the clothes and accessories, which make her look as though she just walked out of the pages of the coolest back-to-school catalog in the world. It's not that in a world that mostly always looks like black and white to me she's like this shocking blaze of color. It's not any of that. It's that with that cloud of long black curls, she's like some sort of dark angel. And it's that when my eyes meet hers, eyes that are the color of a serene ocean, she gives me a quick smile, a nervous smile.

Immediately, I recognize that she's new too, that she's nervous too.

And I recognize something else: I *know* her. I don't mean that we've met before, because we haven't. I don't even know her name! I mean that somehow, instantly, I *know* her.

I've been prepared to say no to everyone all morning, to say "Stay away" to anyone who even *thinks* of drawing near. But as I see her scanning the bus for a friendly face, I start to move my legs, thinking to offer her a seat.

I would give a lot to see that smile again, directed at me.

It may not be much, but I would give everything I've got.

AURORA

In my old school, I used to be in a lot of plays. This meant that my friends all thought I liked getting up on stage, that I didn't mind getting up in front of a large group of people.

That is so not the case.

I like taking lines as they appear flat and two-dimensional on the page and turning those lines into something that breathes life, emotion. I like the scenery, seeing stagehands take naked wood and large sheets of paper or cardboard and transform it all into a forest or a mountain or even someone's private bedroom.

Most of all, I just like acting, hiding behind another personality.

When I stand in front of people as myself, any size group of people, like I'm doing now, I can actually feel the trembling in my legs. *Are people looking at me? Are they staring? Will someone say something that will make me want to crawl under a rock and die?*

The first face I see, outside of the bus driver's, is a friendly one. It's a boy with shaggy hair the color of soft coal and eyes that are the brown of mahogany, turning topaz when whatever morning sun can stream through the grime of the bus windows strikes them. All I notice is his head and that as soon as I smile at him — which is the first thing I do whenever I make eye contact with anybody, just like my mom taught me — his smile is instantly wide open, inviting.

There's something shocking about those topaz eyes — what is

it? — that shakes me to the core, makes me shiver even though it's still so hot out in the mornings this time of year, nails me to the floor where I stand at the head of the aisle.

I'm about to smile again, maybe say, "Hey," when I hear a voice shout to me from somewhere in the middle of the bus.

"Hey!" I hear a girl's voice. "New girl! Come sit back here with us!"

LUCIUS

Two minutes ago, I was hoping no one in this new school would ever notice me, much less talk to me.

A moment ago, I was hoping the Dark Angel would smile at me one more time.

Now she's walking past my seat, headed toward the voice that called out to her.

I told myself before that I wouldn't look back anymore, that I'd just face forward, staring at the bus driver's stringy hair.

But now I can't stop myself from looking back, can't stop myself from watching the Dark Angel's progress.

The Dark Angel doesn't walk like other people do. I'm not sure what the exact word for it is. *Floats? Glides?* No, I don't think there is a word. Who would have guessed it? All those hundreds of thousands of words in the English language — 650,000 to 750,000 words to be exact, not including highly technical and scientific vocabulary — but in the end, language still lets a guy down.

A girl, not Red Ponytail, moves her backpack aside so the Dark Angel can sit down.

"What's your name?" I hear the girl ask.

"Aurora Belle," I hear the Dark Angel answer.

This is the first time I hear her voice. Like her walk, like everything else about her, her voice is different from that of any of the others here. Not a woman's voice exactly, but it is definitely not a girl's voice either. It's soft and low and smoky, but clear as wind chimes somehow.

"You are going to *love* the school!" the girl says, and I wonder if the school board pays her to do public relations. But then I remember: no public relations were leveled in my direction.

"I'm sure I will," Aurora says enthusiastically.

Then everyone around her starts asking her questions all at once: "Where are you from?" "Where did you go to school before this?" "What's your favorite band?"

Up here, I am both a self-exile and an outcast.

But back there?

It is as though I can feel the arms of the entire school reaching out to embrace this Aurora Belle. They want her, want her to be one of them. They want to claim her as part of their pack.

If she were anyone else, I might resent the difference between our receptions.

We are in the same world, but different.

And yet, no, I do not resent this, because there is something just so obviously and basically *good* about this Aurora Belle. She even smiled at me, something no one else in the world would have done this morning.

I want what she has. I want that goodness.

Then I hear what I immediately recognize to be the sound of Shell-Necklace Boy's voice.

"Hey, Aurora Belle," he says with a laziness that does not deceive me, not one bit, "so you're new. I *like* new."

I do not like Shell-Necklace Boy at all. He is trouble.

Back when I was recovering after the explosion, I did a lot

of reading. And, I freely confess, some of that reading was unusual.

One thing that particularly caught my interest was the subject of mercenaries: soldiers for hire. And the type of mercenary that most caught my interest was the Gallowglass.

Gallowglass, which in Irish means "foreign soldiers," were elite military soldiers living in the Western Isles of Scotland and the Scottish Highlands in the thirteenth through sixteenth centuries. They were Scots, but they were also Gaels, meaning they had a common language with the Irish. They were retained by Irish chieftains, sometimes as personal aides, sometimes as bodyguards, because as foreigners the Gallowglass could not as easily be influenced by local feuds.

Imagine the greatest personal protection service you can think of all rolled into one person: that is what it is to be a Gallowglass.

I turn to look at Aurora Belle, see that she is struggling to keep a friendly smile on her face, know that she sees what I see: Shell-Necklace Boy is trouble.

He is the kind of guy who rips the legs off frogs, with no scientific purpose in mind. He is the boy who smiles at your mother and says, "Gee, I'm sorry, Mrs. Wolfe, I told Lucius we shouldn't play catch in your house, but I'm sure he didn't mean to break your favorite lamp," when in fact it was his idea and his lousy throw. He is the kind of guy who every time a girl says no is absolutely positive she must mean yes.

It is amazing how much you can see in other people — the good and the bad, we won't even talk about the ugly — if you just shut up and watch them: watch what they do, listen to what they say, hear how they say it.

I vow, hearing Shell-Necklace Boy continue to speak now to Aurora Belle in his insidious fashion, that I will become her Gallowglass.

Whatever happens, I will stand beside her.

AURORA

I sit here listening to all these new voices swirl all around me and I answer their questions as best I can, smiling brightly, but not too eagerly, all the while. And yet the whole time I'm doing it, beneath the surface I am back with those topaz eyes, more animal than human.

My dad always says that if you can take a thing apart you can understand it, and I try to do that now.

Why did that boy's eyes nail me so like that?

It's not like I'm vain or anything, but I'm aware that guys sometimes check me out. That's just what guys do, and I don't flatter myself to think I'm the only one who draws that kind of attention. And certainly I've had strangers who were guys say hey to me before. Did he say hey? I don't even remember now. Huh. No, I realize, he didn't. I don't even know what he sounds like.

And it's then, when I'm realizing he never said hey and wondering what he sounds like, that it hits me, a bolt:

I have, of course, read about love at first sight. My dad and I are great readers, after all, and he had me reading Shakespeare's comedies, which are always romances too, while my friends were still reading Nancy Drew. So I know all about two people meeting, being instantly attracted, rejecting that attraction and the evidence of their own senses, Cupid wreaking havoc with everything, and everyone somehow ending up in a forest somewhere and getting married before the final curtain. Let me just go on record as saying, my respect for Shakespeare notwithstanding: hogwash. It doesn't happen like that in real life. You don't fall in love with people you've just met for the first time when you don't even know the first thing about them.

And yet here's the scary part, the thing that's like a bolt:

There was an instant *connection*.

When I looked into those topaz eyes, I did feel like I knew him, at least briefly.

But that's still not the scary part; I see that now. The scary part is that in that moment, it was like he knew *me*.

LUCIUS

I'm the first off the bus, feel the warm breeze against my face. What was all that stuff about Gallowglass? I shake my head, like I'm trying to wake myself up. What was all that stuff?

Sometimes I get carried away.

AURORA

I step off the bus with my group of instant friends.

What was all that stuff about a *connection?*

Sometimes I get a little crazy.

"Ready for your first day?" one of my instant friends asks.

I toss my head without thinking about it.

"Of course," I say.

LUCIUS

Weapons-detection devices and hooks are not friends. On the contrary, they are natural enemies.

I know this, and yet somehow, what with the confusion surrounding my encountering the Dark Angel for the first time on the bus, I have forgotten this elemental fact of my new life.

What this means is that when I try to pass through the school's metal detector at the front entrance, red lights go on and an annoying buzzing sound is heard throughout the hallway, the sound echoing off the painted cement-block walls and highly polished linoleum tiles. Those tiles? I'm thinking they won't stay looking highly polished for long. That gun in that security guard's pocket? I'm guessing he's not happy to see me.

Metal detectors: my parents have said that when they were growing up, no schools had these. Of course, my parents also say they used to walk to school in the snow and that gasoline cost something like five cents a gallon. Who knows? Maybe they even say gas stations used to just give it away for free. Parents' memories are never to be completely trusted, just like their repeated advice to "just be yourself." Still, the first few years of my education, none of the schools I went to had metal detectors either. But then kids started getting more violent, or at least more obviously violent, and the world made adjustments.

Violence: these days, it is all the rage.

And now this security guard is feeling some rage too — I can see it in his eyes as he growls at me, "Up against the wall!"

I let my backpack slide to the floor, brace for the coming confrontation.

In my first act of civil disobedience on my first day in my new school, I do not obey, and now I know more acts of civil disobedience are sure to follow.

Seeing my refusal, the security guard frisks me where I stand, arms in the air as he instructs me to raise them. It is a most humiliating position to be in, as the other students stream by, gawking as they go.

I let the security guard feel like he is doing his job, like he is saving the world from a fate worse than death — me — and it is just as he is finishing with patting down my ankles, starting to straighten up to a standing position, that I lower my arms, tap him on the shoulder with one of my hooks.

He jumps at my touch. It's hard to tell if it's from surprise at my daring to touch him or revulsion at what he sees resting on his shoulder now.

I wave both arms in the air, giving him a full three-sixty view of my permanent accessories. "Lots of metal here!" I announce brightly with a shake of the head, flashing all of my teeth. I could be a minstrel saying, "It's *show*time!"

The security guard's face reddens, a mix of anger and embarrassment over his mistake.

For the first time, I look at him closely, see him clearly; funny how your vision can grow cloudy when you're being treated like a criminal when in reality — this time — you didn't even do anything. What I see now is that he's not all that much older than I am, certainly not like the decrepit security guards in my old school who slept more than they watched. This guy's maybe twenty-two, twenty-three, with hair the color of drying straw, large light blue chips for eyes, and a face so pitted with acne scars, it takes a while for it to register that he really is what girls would consider attractive. He's also got a barrel chest that strains his uniform, and he looks like he used to play football in a serious way. I'm seeing a whole story here: someone who maybe had a real shot at the NFL until he blew out his knee.

And now he's here. Sad. He's here in a miserable dead-end job and he just got humiliated on his first day by trying to pat down the school "crip."

And I think I have it bad.

What's that saying about having no feet and meeting someone with no hands and then feeling better about yourself? Or does that go vice versa? Regardless, when you have no hands you always feel sorry for yourself until you meet someone with hands whose life appears to suck even worse than yours does.

Geez. Being a security guard — an end-of-life job — when your whole life is still ahead of you. And I can see from the sharpness in his eyes: he's not stupid. Okay, maybe he's not as bright as I am, but who is? Still, there's a light there, even if life has snuffed the wattage down a bit. He could still have more. But will he ever reach for it?

I feel sorry for him, I think, as I retrieve my backpack from where I dropped it to the floor during the pat down.

I raise my hook to my forehead, give him a salute that I hope he doesn't find insulting even though I do mean it to be slightly ironic — he and I, after all, know each other now — as I begin to head off down the hall.

I glance at him as I pass by, but he doesn't salute back or wave or smile. It's tough to tell what he's thinking now.

Poor guy.

Someone really should have warned him about me.

AURORA

The security guard smiles at me as I pass through the security checkpoint with ease.

This school really is just the nicest place!

LUCIUS

I discover that Shell-Necklace Boy's real name is Jessup Tristan.

I discover this because we are assigned to the same homeroom.

Also here is Red Ponytail, whose real name is Celia Wentworth.

We are all together because our names are clustered at the end of the alphabet. You would think that by now schools would have formed a more sophisticated system for grouping people, but such is the current state of the education system.

"Lucius Wolfe," I hear the teacher call my name.

I have no hand to raise as everyone else has done, so I raise my hook.

"Present," I say from my seat in the corner of the back of the room.

I feel all eyes turn to stare at me, and I feel an almost uncontrollable urge to laugh.

I have heard characters on TV shows say, rudely, "Talk to the hand." I have not always been certain I understand what that means. But now I want to say back to all those staring eyes, "Talk to the hook," and it is all I can do to keep my mouth shut.

The more I keep my mouth shut, my dad keeps telling me, the better off I will be, the less likely to get into trouble.

So, other than the one-word "present," I don't speak at all. I merely raise my right hook to my forehead, tipping an ironic salute to the room at large.

Some days I am all about the ironic gesture.

They already know I have no hands, and some on the bus thought I might be deaf. Now, if I don't speak again, perhaps they'll all forget that "present" and assume I'm mute as well.

A boy can hope.

I see Jessup lean toward Celia, whom I already think of more as his sidekick than anything more, um, romantic, for want of a better word. I think he is going to whisper something stupid, but when he speaks, even though his face and body say *whisper,* his volume says *I want everyone to hear me.*

"Steve was right, on the bus," Jessup says to Celia. "I remember that news story too. This guy with the hooks is definitely the same guy who caused that explosion." He pauses just the barest of seconds before adding, "He *must* be crazy."

You would think this would bother me, but if you thought that, you would be wrong.

So this is to be my designation in my new school: crazy. Everywhere around me, already I see cliques, the kinds of cliques you see in schools everywhere: jocks, troublemakers, mathletes, you name it. Me, I am in a clique unto myself, the sole member of the group called "crazy."

But this is okay with me, I think. Maybe, if Jessup convinces them all that I am crazy, maybe they will all just leave me alone. Maybe they will be too scared to hassle me.

Sometimes it is better to have the world think you are harm*ful* than that you are harm*less.*

I turn away from my classmates to stare out the window and can't prevent a sigh from escaping. I know how many hours remain until the final bell, but I wonder how many minutes are left, how many seconds. If I felt ready to have these people watch me to see how I manage to use a pen, I would get one out plus a sheet of paper right now to do the math. It would be very easy, multiplying the number of hours by sixty minutes, multiplying that by sixty seconds. Hell, why don't I just do it in my head?

Because of the archaic alphabet thing, I assume Aurora Belle is in one of the other homerooms.

I hope wherever she is, people are treating her well.

AURORA

Once I get over my initial nervousness, homeroom is *fun!*

Everyone is so friendly; everyone wants to know all about me.

When a boy named Gary Addams asks what I liked to do in my old school, I tell him I liked to act in plays. So then the girl who invited me to sit next to her on the bus, Deanie Daily, asks what kind of plays.

"I was the Wicked Witch of the West in *The Wizard of Oz*," I say, proud of it. It was my favorite role. Even as a freshman last year, I got major roles in the two productions at my old school.

"I find that hard to believe," Gary says. "I would think you'd have played Dorothy."

I laugh, remembering something.

"After the last performance, after we'd taken off all of our makeup, I ran into this little girl in the bathroom," I say. "She couldn't have been more than four or five. So she asks me, 'Were you in the play?' and I say yes. So she says, 'What part did you play?' and I say, 'What part do you *think* I played?' She stops and thinks about it, and then her eyes light up. She tries to snap her fingers, but hasn't quite mastered that yet, and she cries, 'Toto! You were the little dog!'"

I'm laughing, and now everyone around me is laughing too.

"Here was my big theatrical break, and this little girl" — by now I'm laughing so hard, I can barely gasp the words out — "this little girl thinks I was *the little dog!*"

We're still laughing as we spill out of homeroom and I start trying to figure out where I should be for first period.

As Deanie Daily looks over my course schedule, that boy I saw on the bus this morning walks by, the one who was seated behind the bus driver, the one who was the first kid in this new school to smile at me. Now I see for the first time that he has no hands, has hooks instead.

He smiles at me again, says, "Hey." So this is what he sounds like. I like that sound. There's a solidity to his voice, and yet it also sounds as though he doesn't use his vocal cords very much.

I smile back, say hey back.

"What are you doing, Aurora?" Deanie grabs on to my arm as the boy disappears around the corner.

"What are you talking about?" I say, thinking, *She sure has a tight grip.*

"Why are you saying hello to that guy?" she says, easing up only slightly on my arm. "He's new here, just like you. Before you got on the bus, Steve told us that guy did that *to himself.* Don't you think that's creepy? I think it's creepy. I think *he's* creepy."

Anyone who's ever gone to a school knows that there's never a shortage of rumors, particularly about anyone who's different. The trick is trying to figure out what if any truth lies within the rumors.

"I don't know." I shrug. "I think he seems nice."

"Nice?" I wonder if she's going to need me to help her put her jaw back into place, it's dropped so low. "You think that guy seems *nice?"*

I want to tell her what my mother always taught me: that you should be nice to everyone until a person gives you reason not to be, and sometimes even then.

Back when I was in preschool, there was this boy that was always getting into trouble, T.J. McAllister. Nearly every day, the head of the school, who could be something of a stickler for rules, would make T.J. sit at a table by himself. When we had music, he'd have to go sit in the other room. When we switched sides for art, he'd have to switch, again to go sit by himself. One time he even got left behind when we went on a field trip. I'll admit, some of the things T.J. did were bad. But some of the other stuff? It was all so minor, stuff that all the other kids could get away with every day. The thing was, all the kids started withdrawing from T.J., and after a while, I, T.J.'s last friend in the class, finally pulled away too. It was like he was a disease and we didn't want to catch it.

That's when my mom gave me a talking-to. This was before she got sick.

"How would you like to be T.J.?" she said. "How would you like to always be getting punished for things, even things that are no big deal? How would you like to get left out of the fun stuff, sometimes just for breathing?"

It was something I'd never thought about before: what it must be like to be T.J. It would be awful. Yes, he was louder than the other kids. Yes, he could be obnoxious too, like the time he spat on me for no good reason. Is there ever a good reason to spit on someone else? But it would be awful to be him, I realized. It would feel sad. It would feel lonely all the time.

"Then don't you be like the other kids," Mom said. "I don't care that the head of the school doesn't like T.J. I mean, I care, but I can't do anything about that. And I really can't do anything about how the other kids act. But I can tell you: you should be nicer to him, no matter what anyone else says or does."

She was right, I saw, wondering why I hadn't been able to see it for myself before.

"There are two good reasons," Mom said, "for being nice to the underdogs in this life. One, because if the underdog grows up to be the kind of person that starts shooting, you'll have a chance at survival. Two, because it's the right thing to do." She paused. "Make it three," she added, "the third reason being that the wheel of fortune is always spinning, spinning. And just because you're at the top today doesn't mean it'll always be so. When you're at the bottom, you'll want someone to be there for you too."

I see that wheel spinning now, see how it's just a matter of fortune that has placed me with instant friends on the first day of school while this other new kid is already destined to have none.

But I can't tell Deanie any of that. Somehow, I don't think she'd get it.

So I shrug again. "Yes," I say, hearing the slight note of defiance in my own voice. "I think he seems nice."

Before my mom died, I probably wouldn't have bothered with someone like Deanie. It's so easy to see what she's about: Deanie isn't so much a bad person as that she's the kind of girl who wants to be liked by everybody who's anybody, and that means following the crowd. So if Steve From The Bus says the new guy is bad news, Deanie will give lip service to that. Again, she's not bad; she's just a follower. And me, now that Mom is gone, I guess I've become something of a follower too, or at least too much of a leaf on the wind now to more deliberately choose my own friends.

"I don't know, Aurora." Deanie looks at me funny. "You sure have an odd definition of *nice*. It must mean something different where you come from."

LUCIUS

Already I feel like I'm suffocating in this school, so when open study comes up on my schedule I head outside to the lounge, which is off the cafeteria.

My parents sometimes talk about when they were in school, how outdoor lounges in high school back then were always referred to as the smokers' lounge, where all the smokers in school — students, faculty, security guards — would go to puff away.

Hard to fathom it: the picture of these concrete benches and brick posts being surrounded by a cloud of smoke drifting upward to the overhangs that partially cover the area in case of precipitation. Hard to imagine schools where no one hassled anyone else about smoking, even the underage.

But this campus has signs marking it at the entrance as a "Smoke-Free Zone," and I'll bet if I tried to light up right now, it'd be a hanging offense almost worse than stealing chemicals from the science lab.

I guess it's a good thing for me, then, that I don't smoke.

It's good to be outside, good to feel the fresh air against my skin. For close to the past year, when at home, I'm almost never outside, unless it's to go to and from the car. Still, it's crowded out here, with other kids wanting to take advantage of the sunny weather, and some of those kids are already giving me hard glares as if I'm standing too close to them, as if having no arms might be a catching disease. If this was anything but my first day I might return those glares with one of my best menacing stares, but I just can't take the conflict right off the bat. Besides, a part of me almost feels like, *Who can blame them?*

So I slither through the crowd to a shady corner under one of the overhangs where no one else seems to want to be. I may not get to enjoy the natural sunlight here, but at least there is no one to make me feel like I'm spoiling their day.

It is a fine art, being alone in a crowd.

I'm studying my feet as though they might be the two most interesting things in the world when I hear the sound of a throat being cleared, nervously. Before looking up, I see that two shiny black shoes have moved into my space, and when I do look up, I see the security guard who frisked me this morning.

"I just wanted to say I'm sorry," he says, "about this morning. I guess I was just overeager — first day and all." He clears his throat again. "So, um, I didn't notice."

He indicates my hooks with a jut of his chin, his pockmarked cheeks reddening slightly as he does so.

"S'okay," I say. "People miss these all the time. You know, if I didn't wave them in people's faces, I don't think they'd ever even notice."

His eyes widen, but then he must see I'm just fooling with him and then he actually laughs, a relieved sound, before turning dead serious again.

"So." He gives another one of those chin juts at my hooks. "What happened?"

"Explosion," I say. "Chemicals."

He takes a moment to think about this, as though my two words have painted a big enough picture, then he asks, "How long ago?"

"Not too long into freshman year," I say, adding for clarity, "last year."

He digests this too. He opens his mouth as if to say something else, but no words come out. I understand what he's feeling. What can he possibly say? "I'm sorry"?

There just is no right thing to say. So I save him the futile search by changing the subject.

"How about you?" I ask. "You said this is your first day too. How'd you end up being a security guard at a high school?"

He could easily take this as rudeness on my part, which I wouldn't mind so much, since it would deflect any pity he might be feeling, but he doesn't appear to take it that way.

"Oh, that," he says. "I was supposed to play in the NFL. I actually *made* it to the NFL, but then one day during practice I blew out my knee." His cheeks redden again slightly as he looks down at that offending knee. Then he shrugs. "Game over."

I almost smile. I almost smile because it amazes me how right I can sometimes be about certain people. But I realize in time, before he catches my expression, that just as his "I'm sorry" would have been inadequate to my situation, my amusement would most definitely be insulting to his.

So I show him the same courtesy he showed me: a moment of silence, his in honor of my lost arms, mine in honor of his wrecked knee.

"What's your name?" I ask.

"Nick Greek," he says.

Now I do laugh, a rusty sound.

His eyes narrow. "What's so funny?"

"I don't know," I say. "That's just a funny name."

"Oh, yeah? Is yours any better?"

"Lucius Wolfe," I say.

"No." He laughs for the first time. He sounds like he's had more practice at it than I have. "That sure isn't any better."

It's amazing how you can laugh at something silly with another person, but then as soon as the laughter stops, an awkwardness sets in. I remember that happening sometimes . . . *before*.

"Hey, listen," Nick Greek says. "I know what high school can be like. I mean, I was in high school myself once. And I know what kids can be like." He shoves his hands into the pockets of his navy blue uniform pants and I hear the jingle of loose change as he starts to back away. "So, um, just let me know if anyone gives you a hard time." Then he turns on his heel and saunters away.

Wow, I think. *That is a lot of guilt that guy is feeling just over that one mistake he made this morning.*

He ought to try blowing up his parents' house sometime.

AURORA

"See?" Deanie Daily leans over to whisper in my ear. "I told you that guy was a loser."

I am beginning to think that Deanie Daily could be a Greek chorus all on her own.

We're in the outside lounge, Deanie and I sitting on a brick wall while all around us are a group of other kids I've met today.

I look where Deanie points and see the guy from the bus. He's over in a shady corner by himself — who would choose to stay in the shade on such a sunny day? — with one of the security guards across from him, the guard's back to us.

It's been around school all day, how one of the security guards frisked the guy with no hands first thing in the morning.

"Maybe he's getting in trouble again," Deanie says. "Maybe he's about to get frisked again."

I wish she wouldn't say such things just to make herself look cooler. I wish, at the very least, she wouldn't say them to me.

"I don't think so," I say, feeling the need to defend the guy. "It looks like they're just talking to each other."

In fact, they're doing more than talking together — it looks like they're enjoying each other's company.

"Only losers talk to security guards," Deanie says, unnecessarily.

It's an unnecessary addition because everyone knows this. I refuse to use the word *loser* when talking about another human being, but I do know that in my old school it was only the friendship-challenged kids who ever spent time chatting with the men in blue.

Still, who can blame someone for talking to a security guard — I mean, are security guards lepers or something? — particularly if there's no one else for a person to talk to.

The security guard's back is still to me, but I see the new guy laughing as they're talking. I haven't seen him laugh before this. The sound of that laugh hits my ears from across the lounge. *That laugh,* I think, *could use some practice.*

Then, after a time, the security guard backs away, turns around.

Now the new guy is totally alone over there. With those topaz eyes, it's almost like he's a wolf who's been separated from the pack.

He looks over to where we're all gathered, his eyes catch mine, and the smile he's wearing fades, like the last wisp of smoke from a burned-out fire in the fireplace going up the chimney. What is he thinking?

"C'mon, Aurora," Deanie says. "We're all going inside. Didn't you notice?"

And I am pulled along by the crowd.

LUCIUS

It's my third day of school, my first gym class.

Actually, I should say it's my first day in my second gym class.

I was scheduled to have gym yesterday, but when I arrived I discovered I'd been put in a special PE class with the few kids in school who are in wheelchairs, stuff like that. There were therapists and specialists in the class to help, and we were all supposed to go swimming. Nothing against those kids, but I was annoyed. My disabilities aren't so bad that I can't do what most other kids can do, so before the class even got under way, I went straight to the vice principal's office and demanded a course change. At first I met with resistance. But I've learned that I can be very persuasive when I want to be. Plus, it's amazing how flustered administrators get when you use the words "discrimination" and "lawsuit" in the same sentence. Toss in a few "my civil rights are being violated here," and it's a walk to getting your own way.

My new gym class is now the first period of the day, which I think is absolutely nuts. Isn't it *wrong* somehow to make kids run around when they're still half asleep?

So here I am getting ready for the first gym class that I intend to see all the way through. I'm down in the locker room, taking off my shoes and socks.

I've always thought that communal locker rooms for kids were one of life's little cruelties. Not that it's ever been a problem for me before in that particular regard — meaning being ashamed of what I look like, because, believe me, I had other things about locker rooms to fear — but I can remember the reluctant faces in my old school of heavyset guys as they'd pull their regular shirts over their heads, trying to get their gym T-shirts on almost immediately to avoid having other guys say stuff like, "Hey, fatso," or "Look at lardo!"

Now I know it's my turn to be scrutinized, so I stand in front of my locker, my back to the room, as I use my hooks to strip my shirt up over my head. I'd be lying to myself if I didn't acknowledge what I know is coming my way.

I'm reaching for my gym T-shirt — I made sure to get one with long sleeves — when I hear the voice of Jessup Tristan yell from behind me, "Hey! New guy!"

I ignore him as I take hold of the T-shirt.

"Hey, new guy!" he yells even louder. "I'm talking to you!"

"My name is Lucius Wolfe," I say, still keeping my back to him.

"Fine," he says. "Hey, Wolfe!" As he says my name, I feel a rather aggressive towel strike against my exposed back like a terrycloth whip.

I turn, T-shirt in hand, and see Jessup standing there with a couple of guys I recognize: Gary Addams, who so far hasn't seemed too bad, and Steve, whose last name I don't know but who I remember as the guy who first started talking about me that first day on the bus.

Of course, when I turn, they see my chest. They see the skin discolorations, the railroad tracks of scars that meander all over it. My face the doctors did a good job on. My chest, not so much.

Gary and Steve look queasy.

"Whoa!" Jessup says, holding up an arm as though to shield his eyes from a too-bright sun. "Put a shirt on over that thing!"

Then he changes his mind. "Hey!" he says to the room at large. "Get a load of Frankenstein over here!"

Idiot, I think. *He doesn't even know that Frankenstein is just the name of the doctor who* created *the monster.*

"That's the Frankenstein monster to you," I say, dropping the T-shirt on the ground and raising my hooks like Boris Karloff trying to scare off a whole village of idiots.

It's astonishing how satisfying it feels to see Jessup briefly recoil in fear.

But Jessup's not my little sister, Misty, and he is not the sort to be kept down for long. Worse luck, me.

"Hey," he says, as I'm pulling on my gym shorts, "how do you jerk off with those things?"

Funny he should ask.

Yes, guys our age — news flash! — jerk off. I suspect guys of all ages do, pretty much from the age they first figure out that the thing they pee with is capable of doing other things right up until the day they get so old they forget what it's for again. We all do that thing that people used to warn boys not to do, saying it would make them go blind. We do it, in fact, because we're *hoping* to temporarily go blind. In a way, at least.

All I'll say on the subject?

It does present its challenges.

Life is full of challenges, made more difficult when a person does something stupid, like blowing off his own hands.

Guys our age also fantasize all the time about being with girls.

Unless of course we fantasize about being with other boys, but I'm not part of that second *we,* no offense to anyone who is.

Actually, I've been fantasizing about girls for pretty much as long as I can remember. But I always knew it was fantasy, with no basis in reality. I mean, it's not as if I was ever what you'd call a real popular guy in my old school, not even before I blew my own hands off.

Hell, I've never even kissed a girl.

But I have had my crushes and my fantasies. I have had those. And I even used to dream that one day fantasy would become reality. But how is that possible now?

I've tried to imagine what that would be like now if it ever did finally happen: being with a girl — you know, *really* being with her. How would I touch her the way a guy is supposed to?

Even the most basic things are mind-boggling. For example, I know everyone's supposed to use condoms these days. It's the thing to do unless you're — oh, I don't know — older and trying to make a baby. In fact, I'm pretty sure it was the thing to do even back in my parents' day — you know, that despite smokers' lounges, walking to school in the snow, free gas, and people liking you if you "just be yourself," condoms were the way to go. But how would the logistics of such a thing work?

Believe me, I have given this a lot of thought. And all I can think is, either I'd poke a hole in the condom with my hook or I'd be so nervous and excited and eager, I'd accidentally cut off my own penis with my pincers while trying to roll the condom on.

Yes, for some lucky girl I will be a real prize . . .

I look at Jessup steadily, Jessup with his penchant for asking questions about jerking off. I know, through hard experience, that the steadier you can look at a bully once he's really decided to go after you, the more likely he is to back down.

Disaster does have a tendency to teach a person a few things.

Before blowing my hands off, I was the kind of kid who always kept his eyes averted, looking to avoid trouble. This meant that trouble had no problem finding me at all and I spent more than one morning getting tripped in the halls, more than one lunch period locked in a locker because someone had shoved me there, more than one afternoon gym class in which someone gave me a decidedly unpleasant wedgie.

Of course, I'm a lot bigger than I was back then, have grown a lot in the past year. Hey, if I'd known blowing off my hands would somehow coincide with my transforming from Wimpy Guy into Strong Guy, maybe I'd have mixed up that chemical cocktail and blown them off sooner.

"Very carefully," I answer Jessup. "Very carefully."

AURORA

"My dad says that new guy, the one with the hooks, insisted on being in a regular gym class," Celia Wentworth says, redoing her ponytail and giving her head a little toss so that the red hair bounces like soft copper under the fluorescent lights of the locker room. I don't like to be critical, but I don't think I've ever quite seen a girl get so much mileage out of a ponytail before, the way she's always tossing that thing around.

It turns out that Celia Wentworth's dad is the vice principal.

"And guess which regular gym class got lucky?" she continues.

As I change into my gym shorts, I can tell she's expecting me to agree with her, that this is somehow the end of the world. But I say nothing.

"Well," she sighs, "at least we have Jessup in our class. I think Jessup's cute. Don't you think Jessup's cute?"

"Definitely," Deanie agrees with her, nodding like a bobblehead.

Again, I say nothing.

But inside I am thinking that if Deanie is obsessed with doing and saying whatever it takes to be liked by everybody who is anybody, then Celia is obsessed with doing and saying whatever it takes to be liked by just one person: Jessup Tristan.

LUCIUS

You have to wonder about a gym teacher who thinks volleyball is the ideal sport for the first day of gym class. And you really have to wonder about a gym teacher who thinks having teams be girls against the guys is some kind of wonderful and novel idea. I have a particular gripe with this, since it lands me on a team with Jessup, Steve, Gary, and two other guys. Across the net from us are Aurora, Celia, Deanie, and three other girls. There's another twelve kids playing a game at a second net set up crosswise on the other half of the basketball court.

Before class started, the gym teacher, Mrs. Finch, pulled me aside and tried to convince me that playing volleyball with the others might not be such a good idea for me. She thought it might be beyond my abilities or that maybe I'd get hurt. So I pulled out the words "discrimination" and "lawsuit" and the phrase "my civil rights are being violated here," and before you know it, I was in the game.

I briefly consider becoming a lawyer when I grow up. I think I have the basics down pat here.

I have to admit, playing volleyball the first day of gym class and being on an all-boys team isn't all bad: it means I can keep an eye on Aurora on the other side of the net. She looks so pretty in her gym clothes, the pale green and white making her hair look that much darker, making her eyes stand out that much more.

Even though Jessup complains that it's sexist, Mrs. Finch lets the girls serve first.

I'm paying too much attention to how Aurora looks as she goes up on her toes, tossing the ball up in the air with one hand and then elongating her whole body to serve it with the other, to notice much of anything else. Which is okay, because the ball doesn't come to me anyway. I'm in the back row and nowhere near close to it as it comes down in the center on our side of the net. Good thing, because while I might not care about what most people think, I'd feel like an idiot if during the first play of the game Aurora saw me take the ball in the head because I wasn't paying sufficient attention.

Eye on the prize: sometimes it is a challenge.

The game progresses and it doesn't take long before I notice something odd about this game: no one is hitting the ball to me. Not the other side, not any of my teammates. I doubt it was intentional on Aurora's part when she served — I just can't see her doing that — but when none of the other girls hits the ball in my direction, no matter what position the rotation of play puts me in, I remember Mrs. Finch huddling with the girls before the game started. Call me paranoid, but I become convinced Mrs. Finch warned them not to hit the ball anywhere near me. She was probably worried, didn't want a student getting injured on her watch.

Apparently now Mrs. Finch has become concerned about other kinds of lawsuits.

It makes me angry.

But then Aurora is serving again, Mrs. Finch is at the other end of the court supervising the other game, and this time the ball is coming straight at me. It's mine. My feet leave the ground as I reach to bang the ball back with the side of my prosthetic arm — it's amazing how powerful these things can be.

Before I can make contact, though, I feel a body slam into me, hard, from the left, sending me crashing to the ground. I look up just in time to see Jessup fly across my field of vision as he steals my play. He hits the ball with so much force right down the center, none of the girls on the other side even has a chance of returning it.

"What was that all about?" I demand from my position on the floor.

"Sorry, dude." He shrugs, like *No harm, no foul.* "I was just trying to do you a favor."

"Well, don't," I say.

I really hate, have always hated, to have anyone call me *dude*.

"Sorry, dude," he says again, like he means it. Then he surprises me by reaching out a hand to help me up.

Not thinking — I still forget sometimes that I don't have hands anymore, particularly when I'm dreaming at night, such wonderful dreams — I raise my hook to take it.

Jessup sees what I'm offering and he takes a step backwards, raises his hands as though to ward off evil.

"Oops," he says, "I forgot." Then his eyes light up like he's just thought of something great. "Hey!" he says, continuing in a soft voice meant just for me to hear. "I never can seem to remember your name. What was it again? Luke Wooly? Lucy Whales? So why don't I just call you 'Hooks' from now on?" He nods to himself. "Yeah. It's perfect: Hooks."

Well, I think as I rise to my feet, *no one could have seen* that *coming.*

"I swear, Hooks," he says, "I really was just trying to help the team make the play. You know, you really should be in the special needs gym class or something, maybe not even take gym at all. I mean, what were they thinking, putting you in here with normal people?"

"You'd be surprised what I can do with these hooks," I tell him.

And it's true. I can do some amazing things, such as shoot pool like nobody's business. First thing my dad did when we moved into the new house: he bought a new table to replace the one we lost in the explosion. First thing I did when I was well enough: I taught myself how to play pool all over again. It's amazing what a natural bridge hooks make.

But I don't tell Jessup any of that. What does he care about what I have to say? Instead, I show him.

On the next play, it is finally, at last, my turn to serve.

I consider waiting for my second serve to do what I'm going to do, but then I decide: Nah. Why wait?

I bend my knees to get a good spring jump, then I toss with my left, but when I strike with my right I don't even try to get it over the net. Instead, I use all my power to zero in on my real target: the unsuspecting back of Jessup, who's standing right in front of me.

"Ow!" he cries, his back arching against the pain I've just inflicted.

"Oops," I say when he turns to glare at me. "Sorry . . . *dude.*" I wave my hooks in the air innocently. "Sometimes I don't know what I'm doing with these things, you know?"

Violence: these days it really is all the rage.

AURORA

"God, can you believe that new guy?" Celia says when we're back down in the locker room. "I couldn't believe it when he spiked Jessup with the ball like that. It was totally on purpose."

"I know," Deanie agrees with her. "Personally, I think he's crazy. I mean, why else would he even *have* hooks? Don't they have much more modern prosthekits these days?"

I want to tell her that the proper word is *prosthetics,* but I don't. And yes, I'm sure Lucius spiked Jessup on purpose. But I'm also equally sure that when Jessup crashed into Lucius earlier, it was no innocent accident. Still, what Deanie said has me curious now, and rather than going to study hall like I'm supposed to after gym, I go to the library instead to see if my dad can help me with a little research.

—"Hey, princess," my dad says when he sees me. "What can I do for you? Is this business or pleasure?"

This is the first time I've visited my dad in the library and I can tell from what he's said at home that he's settling in to his new job nicely. He's said that the staff is mostly friendly and that none of the kids has given him any real trouble yet: no one engaging in extreme forms of PDA among the stacks, no one trying to break the security walls and access porn on the Internet, no one even talking too loudly. This makes me glad. The last few years have been so hard on him, so it's a relief to see that at least one thing is turning out to be easy.

"I need some help with some research," I answer his question.

"Ah, business then," he says. He turns to his computer, fingers poised over the keys. "What'll it be?"

"I want to learn about prosthetics. Specifically, I'd like to know if there's a good reason someone would have a pair of hooks instead of those more advanced prosthetics you see on TV — you know, like on all those soldiers coming home from Iraq."

My dad gives me a quick look, but then he turns his attention back to the keys and begins tapping away. I understand the look: this school may be way bigger than the last high school I went to, but you can't miss the only double amputee, and you really can't miss the only boy with two hooks for hands.

It takes my dad a couple of minutes, but then I see the "Ah-ha!" look he always gets on his face when he locates the answer to something he's been curious about.

He turns the screen so it's facing more toward me, but he's a quicker reader than I am and he starts paraphrasing out loud.

"This article is about soldiers wounded in Iraq," he says. "It focuses on this one double-arm amputee who uses what they call traditional metal hook prosthetics. It says he was told the myo-electric — battery-operated — hands would be the best thing for him. But he was disappointed. He says — get this! — that what the article refers to as 'World War II–era technology' is better, easier: they don't fall off his arm like the other kind is prone to do, and the hooks are more supple and reliable. Oh, and look at this: it says that most single-arm amputees prefer not to use any device at all, because all the devices are too heavy — they don't have the support of natural arms — but when a person is a double-arm amputee, he doesn't really have a choice. Wow! This guy they're talking about in the article can drive a car, shoot a rifle, handle a bayonet, and even teach martial arts with his hooks!"

"But if all that is true," I say, "then why would anyone ever opt for those myoelectric ones you mentioned?"

"Cosmetics," my dad says right away. "They look more like real hands. Most people, I guess, care what other people think. And maybe that's why the soldiers we see on TV almost always have the prosthetics that look more like real hands even though hooks are more effective: because whoever picks what vets to show on TV wants the audience to see something that on the surface looks prettier than reality."

My dad removes his glasses, rubs his eyes. He spends so much time in front of a computer, he often gets eye strain and headaches.

"I suppose there could be other reasons too, individual case by individual case," he says, putting his glasses back on.

"Like what?" I ask.

He shrugs. "Like insurance. I'll bet the more advanced prosthetics would be a lot more expensive, and if coverage wasn't good, or if a person had no medical insurance at all, a person might choose a less expensive option. Then, too, I'd imagine if a person was young when he got injured, he'd outgrow the more advanced prosthetics more quickly. Boys grow a lot between the ages of, say, fourteen and adult. Lower arms and mechanical hands that look fine size-wise on a boy would start looking disproportionate more quickly than hooks as the boy ages into a man. So again, hooks would be a cheaper option because of that." His face has a thoughtful expression. "And there could be other reasons a person would make that choice."

"Such as?"

He shrugs. "I suppose there could be reasons that would be impossible for other people to know."

It's a lot to think about.

"Thanks, Daddy," I say.

"Is there anything else I can help you with? Is there anything else you'd like to know? You know," he says, gesturing at the computer, with a smile, "I really am pretty good with this thing."

Yes, there is something else I would like to know, badly.

I'm dying to know more about what really happened to Lucius.

How hard would it be for my dad to find out? After all, I've heard the other kids say they remember seeing something about it in the city newspaper. So it can't have been that long ago; it can't have been that far away. In the space of a few minutes, with a few keystrokes, my dad can probably get the whole story. What would that story reveal?

And yet, I can't bring myself to ask him to do that. It feels as though I'd be invading Lucius's privacy somehow.

"No, thanks." I shake my head hard, as though trying to convince myself. "That's it for today."

———

Out in the hallway, right outside the library door, Jessup is leaning against the wall.

"Hey," he says. He hooks a finger at the library door. "What were you talking about with that weird guy?"

"You mean *the librarian?*" I say.

He nods.

"That 'weird guy' happens to be my father," I say hotly.

"Oops." He smiles, doesn't really look embarrassed. "Sorry. I guess I just think that all teachers, or people who have jobs that make them seem like teachers, are kind of weird."

"It must make life a lot simpler," I say, "to make generalizations about whole groups of people when you know nothing about the individual."

I move to walk past him, but he springs in front of me, blocking my way.

"So, um." He does this thing where he snaps both sets of fingers, then takes the thumb-side fist of one hand and slaps it against the other hand's open palm. He does it again. "Walk you to your next class?"

"You're kidding, right?" I say.

He just raises his eyebrows, looking genuinely surprised, like he expected me to say yes.

"Um, no," I say, finally succeeding in snaking around him.

It's then I see Celia waiting halfway down the hall. I think she's waiting for me, but then I hear her call out, "Jessup? You coming?"

Even though Jessup can be a jerk, causing me to keep reminding myself of what my mom said about being nice to everybody, he's still a part of the group that I've been . . . *absorbed into* here, for lack of a better way to put it. So when lunchtime rolls around, even though I could do with a little less time around Jessup, I still sit at the table he's at because that's where Celia and Deanie and Steve and Gary are. Plus, each day they yell for me to come sit with them. The things they talk about don't tend to interest me much, mostly just gossip about other people. Mostly, I just keep quiet when they do this.

It's when I'm going up to dump the rest of the stuff left on my orange tray into the trash basket that I run into Lucius.

I've noticed that Lucius always eats by himself.

When he doesn't say anything, when he just dumps the stuff off his own tray and starts to turn away, I say softly, "Hey, Lucius."

You can almost hear the snap as he turns sharply to look at me. Immediately, I realize he's surprised that I know his real name.

He coughs, then: "Aurora." He says it like a statement. And suddenly I'm surprised that he knows *my* name.

"I was just wondering," I say, "are you okay? I mean, that was a pretty big fall you took in gym class this morning. It must have hurt."

This is the most I've ever said to him. Who am I kidding? All we've ever said to each other before was "Hey." Did I say too much?

I realize I must have said too much, because his eyes darken with . . . *something*.

"I'm fine." He practically growls the words. "I'm fine."

Then he's walking away from me, raising a hook to punch open one of the cafeteria doors.

I look back at the table where I've been sitting, catch Jessup looking at me. There's a split second before he realizes I'm looking back at him, and in that split second before he plasters a smile on his face, I see him looking at me with something in his eyes that I don't have a name for.

I just know I don't like it.

LUCIUS

Two weeks have passed and, so far, I have survived.

I spend my Saturday morning doing laundry. This is something I do whenever I have free time now. My mom, seeing how frequently I make trips to the basement laundry room, has offered to do this for me. I think she worries that I'm turning into an obsessive-compulsive, or that maybe I'm down here trying to transform the washing machine into a bomb. But I don't let her do my laundry. I say she has enough of her own work to do. My obsessions are my own. I want my stiff jeans to fade, get softer. I may not care, generally speaking, what others think, but my stiff jeans make me feel like a dork. Vanity, thy name is sometimes Lucius.

I'm transferring the wash into the dryer when I hear Misty's tread on the stairs. Even though she makes every effort to be a bratty sister and daughter — I sometimes think it's a role she's learned from watching too much TV — her footsteps are cheerily distinctive, containing a bounce that is nothing like my parents' tired footsteps. I glance up to see her slouching in the doorway of the laundry room. She looks bored or something.

"What's going on?" I say.

"Wanna shoot pool?" she offers, not really answering my question.

"Sure, just let me finish this," I say. I finish loading the dryer, hookload by hookload, use my hook to set the dial at seventy minutes, use my hook to depress the button.

I go through the door of the laundry room, then pass through my dad's home office at the base of the stairs — thankfully, he's not there — and into the rec room, where Misty is waiting for me, balls racked, cue stick already chalked.

I was a much better pool player than Misty before the accident and, having put much effort into recovering my game, I am once again.

I sometimes think that whoever invented hooks for hands, that person must have been someone who loved pool. How else could he have designed a device that performs so perfectly at the game?

"Do you want to break, or shall I?" I ask, taking a twenty-one-ounce stick out of the wall rack and chalking it until the tip is coated in that perfect sky blue, blowing the excess dust off the tip. It sparkles briefly in my field of vision, hanging in the air before drifting down to the brick red linoleum floor.

"Me," Misty says, bending over to line up the cue ball in her favorite spot: just an inch in from the right bank, so far forward that it's flirting with a violation of being over the break line.

I've tried to tell her before that this is an insane position to break from, that you can't get enough power from it, that it's too easy to scratch the shot, but she never listens. Misty can be stubborn that way.

I know what she's thinking when she breaks, know why she opted to break herself rather than letting me take it: she knows that this way at least she has a chance to sink a few shots before I take over the game. She knows I've become such a bionic pool player that if *I* break, there's a fair chance I'll run the whole table.

Who wants to lose without ever even being in the game?

Misty does pretty well. She doesn't scratch on the break, managing to sink two balls: a solid and a stripe. It's her choice, and she goes for solids, training her stick on the maroon seven. She sinks it no problem, but then she blows an easy tap shot on the blue two, groaning as she cedes the table to me.

I study the remaining twelve balls, plotting how I can sink all six of the striped balls left plus the eight.

People think to be a good pool player all you need do is put a ball in the pocket, like hitting a ball over the fence in baseball or a tiny ball into a tiny cup in golf. But there's so much more to it than that. In order to be really good, you need to be able to see the shot after the shot you're taking right now; to be great, you have to see how to strategize in order to clean the whole table. Pool is a game of concentration and angles, yes, but it's also a game of looking to the leave: *If I do this, where does it leave me? If I take this shot, what angle do I need to come at it from not only to make my shot but also to set myself up for where I want to be for my next shot? Oh, and by the way, if I sink all my balls, what's the point of my accomplishment if I manage to stitch myself on the eight?*

To avoid that last problem, I've lately taken to working the games I shoot backwards in my brain, meaning I think first about how I want to come at the eight in the end, before working backwards in my mind, step by step through each ball and angle it's going to take me to get there until I arrive at the first ball that needs to be conquered.

But I don't do any of that higher-level playing right now as I face off against Misty. I sense there's something she wants to discuss with me but that she won't get the chance if I run the table on her. So I go for the long orange thirteen striper — picking a table-length shot, so she won't get suspicious — but instead of sinking it smoothly and with authority like I can, I tap it just enough off center to cause it to bounce off the pointed corner of the bank.

"Darn," I say, shaking my head as though amazed at my own ineptitude. If I still had fingers, I would snap them here to emphasize my dismay at my own lack of finesse. As it is, I have to settle for shuffling my feet and staring at my cue as though it's somehow offended me.

"I chalked this thing, didn't I?" I say.

Misty rolls her eyes at me. "Of course you did. Aren't you the one who's always telling me 'chalk is cheap' and that I have to remember to chalk my own cue between each shot?"

"That does sound like me," I say, and for once, even though it's so rare for me, I can't help but grin.

Misty studies the table, doesn't grin back.

"So, how's the new school working out for you?" I ask Misty as she takes her turn. I figure, she's a kid, she's always been a far more social kid than I am, so what else could be on her mind?

"There's this boy in my class," she says, "Bobby Parker."

"There's always a Bobby Parker," I say.

She looks at me, puzzled by my wit.

I sigh. "What did this particular Bobby Parker do?" I ask.

"He somehow learned about you," she says. "He told me he thinks you're crazy."

"And what did you say in response?" I ask, sure of the answer.

Surely she will have agreed with this Bobby Parker: Misty's brother is a nutcase, a whackaloon. Good citizens would be well advised to hide all the women and chickens.

"I told him if he didn't shut up about it," she says, "I'd sic you on him and then he'd see how crazy you really were." She looks at me like she's worried I'll yell at her. "Was that okay?"

I try not to let the huge smile I'm feeling on the inside show on my face. "I'm not sure that threatening your fellow classmates with me visiting upon them grievous bodily harm is the best way to convince them that I'm not the craziest person in town," I say sternly. But then I just can't help it: the smile breaks across my face. "But yes," I add, "what you told Bobby Parker was perfectly all right. Just don't make a habit of it."

She heaves a sigh of relief, and I think how I can't believe this: my little sister has stood up for me.

"It must be hard on you," I say, sobering, "having everyone in school think your brother is crazy, maybe even acting as though you must be just like him. I'm sorry."

She shrugs. "It's not really that bad." Then she laughs. "I mean, at least they're not *all* Bobby Parkers."

We share a chuckle moment now that she has at last grasped my earlier joke.

"Really, aside from Bobby Parker," she says, "I've made a ton of friends." Now it's her turn to sober. "Anyway," she says, "it must be even harder on you."

"Not really." I shrug, not wanting her pity. "So tell me about this ton of friends." *Ton of friends* — it's a foreign country to me.

I listen as Misty excitedly tells me about girls with names like Kiki, Tiki, and Biki.

"*Biki?*" I say. "Did someone actually name their kid *Biki?* What is *wrong* with some of these parents?"

I mock that which I don't understand while wondering at the world Misty and Aurora live in, an astonishing world in which a person can make a ton of new friends instantly without even appearing to try, an unimaginable world in which a person actually expects to make a ton of friends and can even do so by following that insane advice to "Just be yourself."

"How about you?" she asks. I can tell right away that she knows exactly where my mockery comes from, see the pity in her eyes. "Have you made any friends in your new school?" She poses the question cautiously, as though she expects the answer to be obviously negative.

"One," I say. "Maybe."

Misty raises her eyebrows at me, a look of shock and an invitation to tell her more.

I think of Aurora. I think about the evidence I see before my very eyes every day in the cafeteria: Celia liking Jessup, Jessup liking Aurora, Aurora liking . . . who? I think how, even though I was a jerk to her that first time she tried to talk to me in the cafeteria, and even though I'm still often a jerk to her, it hasn't stopped her from saying hey to me every time she sees me in the halls — who knew that having someone else simply say hey to a person could feel like such a big deal, could become the high point of a person's every day? My being a jerk hasn't stopped her from smiling at me each time she says hey, sometimes even going further to ask how I'm doing whenever we're in the same place for more than a second. She is the only person in the school, including teachers, who is constantly nice to me.

I am not used to other people being kind.

And, since I am still frequently a jerk to her, responding to her overtures with terse one-word answers, I wonder why she bothers. And yet I can't help the way I act around her. I was terse with her that first day in the cafeteria because I didn't want her pitying me, because I had no idea how to handle someone being *nice* to me for a change — it had been so long — and now I don't know how to stop. I'm like a prickly pear, and yet Aurora can't seem to stop herself either, can't seem to stop being nice to me.

"Maybe," I say again to Misty. "Maybe."

I see another look of pity cross her face. In Misty's social world, where more is always by definition better, it must seem pathetic: the idea of a person having only one "maybe" friend.

We finish out the game.

I let her win.

And afterward, for good measure, I let her beat me again.

AURORA

It's become habit for my dad and me to go to Angelo's Pizza for Sunday night dinner.

The idea was all mine.

I told my dad that he slaves over a hot stove six days a week, and that he deserves a day of rest. I told him I had no intention of learning to cook in order to provide him with that day of rest. I told him I'd even pay for these Sunday night dinners using my allowance money.

My dad has given me a weekly allowance for as far back as I can remember. The amount is always equal to that of my age. I get to keep eighty percent of it, while ten percent goes to savings and ten percent goes to charity. This means I now get fifteen dollars a week from which I get to keep twelve. Since I don't spend a lot, it tends to pile up. For this money, I don't have to do a thing except "be a member of this family," as my dad puts it. He says that all family members are shareholders in the wealth.

There is a good reason why, where we used to live, my friends thought my dad was the greatest dad who ever lived.

Oh, and if I do want extra money for something special? My dad says I can always do chores to earn that. But I almost never want anything and I do chores anyway, telling my dad that "shareholder" shouldn't have to mean "lazy and useless."

My dad resisted my offer to spring for pizza — "I think I can afford to feed my own daughter, princess" — but I insisted.

And so we go early each Sunday night to Angelo's, where, amid the heavenly aromas of rolled dough, fresh tomatoes, and melted string cheese, we discuss books and life.

As we wait for our pizza, I sip at my Coke. My dad won't let me drink diet soda. He says he can't stop me from rotting my teeth with regular soda the way other kids do, but he refuses to let me put chemicals in my body that he finds suspect. My dad also has written up his unpublished theory that diet products make people fat. *Show me a fat person,* it opens, *and I'll show you a fridge stocked with diet soda.*

I don't really see that regular soda is any better for a person than diet soda — and I suppose my dad isn't saying it's any good either, only that he finds it to be the better of two evils — but if it makes him moderately happier to see me consume 150 calories more per can, I'm game.

"So," my dad asks, "how's school going so far?"

You would think, with us being in the same school every day, we'd talk about it all the time at home. But my dad believes in giving me space and I believe in giving him space too, so after the first few days, we stopped asking each other all the time.

"It's good," I say truthfully. "You know, it's funny. I was sure I'd have trouble fitting in. I was so used to my friends in my old school. But everyone here has really been so welcoming."

"I'm glad," my dad says. "Anyone in particular?"

"Well," I say, "there's Deanie and Celia. Deanie can be a little wishy-washy about some stuff" — I wrinkle my nose at the thought of some of her wishy-washiness — "but she is really friendly. And Celia?" I think about this one a little longer. "She's mostly very nice to me. But sometimes, I wonder if she just does it because Jessup Tristan does. I think she likes him."

"Ah, Mr. Tristan," my dad says.

"What does that mean?" I ask.

But he doesn't answer. Instead he says, "What do you think of Mr. Tristan?"

"I'm not sure," I say. "Sometimes, I think he acts *too* nice to me, like it's false somehow, but I don't know."

I think about what Jessup said to me the day after I ran into him outside the library, when he said he thought the new librarian was odd before realizing the librarian was my dad. The next day he apologized again, but it was a weird kind of apology.

"I'm sorry," he said with a laugh. "I just always thought it was strange for *anyone* to want to be a librarian, but particularly for a *guy* to want to be one. Know what I mean?"

"No, I don't," I told him evenly.

But then he told a joke about something else — Jessup can actually be quite funny when he's not making fun of someone — and I forgot all about it for a while.

"I know what you mean," my dad says now. "One day I realized one of the students had done something to the computers so that a site could be viewed that the school doesn't, um, allow." My dad's cheeks color slightly, so I know he must be talking about porn. Parents get worked up about both sex and violence, but I have noticed they never blush when talking about violence. "I could have sworn," my dad goes on, "that Mr. Tristan was the only one who used that computer that day, but when I checked the sign-in log, it was another kid's signature. That student I was sure *hadn't* used the library at all that day, but when I asked him to write out his signature for me, it was a match. Naturally, I couldn't turn in a phantom, so I just reprogrammed the settings on the computer and I had to let the matter drop."

"Weird," I say. "Kind of creepy too."

Our pizza comes, but it's too hot to eat right away. It's the veggie special, my dad's doing. He says this will counteract the harm done by the sugar in my soda. So he doesn't feel bad, I pretend I'm excited about the prospect of eating eggplant and olives rather than pepperoni and double cheese.

I know my dad tries too hard at, really, everything. But I also know nothing is easy on him anymore, feeling like he has to be both dad and mom. Nothing has been easy on him for a very long time.

My dad bites into a slice too soon, burning the roof of his mouth.

"You know," he says, after downing half my Coke to soothe the sizzle on his tongue, "Mr. Tristan reminds me of the Mr. Bubble boy."

"The who?"

"He was a kid who used to come into your Grandpa Aaron's store every day."

Grandpa Aaron owned his own pharmacy for most of my dad's childhood, until all the CVSes and stuff took over. My dad sometimes tells stories about helping Grandpa Aaron restock the candy, ring the register — back, he always reminds me, before registers told you how much change to give, when human beings could still add and subtract in their very own heads — and sometimes even count out pills for prescriptions when no one was looking.

I at last take a bite of my own first slice. Truth time: I actually do like the way the mushrooms, onions, and peppers interact with the stringy hot cheese. The eggplant does make whatever it touches a little watery, but the olives always remind me of my mom. Mom loved her olives.

"So what did this Mr. Bubble boy do?" I ask, not taking the time to totally swallow first.

"Like I say," my dad says, "this boy used to come in every day. And every day he'd shout out a big, friendly 'Hi, Mr. Belle!' to your grandfather."

"What's wrong with that?" I want to know.

"Nothing, in and of itself," my dad says. "But when I was growing up, there was this wonderful product on the market called Mr. Bubble. I don't know if they even still make it anymore. They probably do, only now I'll bet they make it in a liquid form and put it in a plastic bottle."

I wait while my dad has a nostalgia moment.

Sometimes I wonder what I will feel nostalgic for when I'm his age. Some days I feel as though I'm already nostalgic for so much, every memory I have filed under either Before Mom Got Sick or After.

"Anyway, the Mr. Bubble *I* grew up with," my dad continues, "was in powder form and came in this *humongous* pink and white box."

I swear, when my dad tells these stories about his childhood, sometimes he seems like he's still a kid. If he knew about the word *ginormous,* he'd probably use it to describe that Mr. Bubble box. Still, his sudden excitement is contagious and I feel myself get eager, hopeful for a good story coming my way.

"It was a bubble bath," my dad answers my silent question. "Mr. Bubble made the biggest bubbles. They gave the best bath."

"Um, sounds really wonderful." I can't believe he's stopped the flow to do a commercial spot. "But what does any of this have to do with the Mr. Bubble boy?"

"I'm getting to that, I'm getting to that." He waves his pizza slice at me as though he's mad at my interruption, even though I know he's not. He does look a bit surprised, though, when his pizza waving causes all the toppings and cheese to slide right off his slice. At last he shrugs it off. "So there was this kid, coming in to say hi to my dad every day. 'Hi, Mr. Belle!' Truth? Sometimes I was jealous of him, because my dad was always telling me what a great little boy he was, such good manners. Hey, I always shook hands when I met new people, I was always polite to the customers. But then one day my dad catches this kid stealing a giant box of Mr. Bubble. And, after just the mildest questioning on my dad's part — he swore there were no thumbscrews involved — the kid spills that he's been stealing a box of Mr. Bubble every day and selling it on the bubble black market at school."

"The *bubble* black market?" I can't help it. I'm laughing hard now.

"Hey!" My dad looks mildly offended. "Back when I was a kid, we didn't have GameBoys and Nintendos and all this high-tech stuff you do. We were lucky to have Mr. Bubble!" But he can't help it: now he's laughing too.

"But how could Grandpa Aaron not have known what was

going on?" I ask my dad. "Didn't you say that those, um, Mr. Bubble boxes were huge? You know, like, *ginormous?*"

"Gi-*what?*" He shrugs. "The Mr. Bubble boy probably just shoved it under his T-shirt as soon as your grandpa got busy filling prescriptions. Besides, back then — you know, in the dark ages of pre-civilization known as 'my youth' — we didn't have high-tech security systems either. No video cameras — my dad didn't even have a security *mirror* until well into my teens."

"But what did Grandpa Aaron think was happening to all that Mr. Bubble before he caught the kid?"

My dad shrugs. "I guess he just figured it was his biggest seller." My dad slides another slice of pizza onto his plate, pauses to ponder something. "I wonder what ever happened to Bobby Parker?"

"Who's that?" I ask.

"The Mr. Bubble boy. I just remembered, his name was Bobby Parker." Then he shrugs again. "Who knows? Bobby's probably in Sing Sing by now, doing time for grand theft auto . . . or worse. And yet for some reason, your Mr. Tristan reminds me of him."

"He's not *my* Mr. Tristan," I say, while inside I'm thinking, *But I think he wants to be.* "And why does he remind you of the Mr. Bubble boy?"

"All those cheerful days of 'Hi, Mr. Belle!' that Bobby Parker gave my dad, when in reality he was committing crimes. I just get the feeling that Mr. Tristan does the same thing: smiles in people's faces, when in reality he's doing . . . who knows what?"

"I guess it's a good thing he's not the guy I like then, isn't it?"

"There's a guy you like?" My dad nearly drops his whole slice of pizza this time and not just the toppings.

Uh-oh. Now I've really put my foot in it.

I feel my cheeks reddening. "Not *like* like," I insist, hoping my dad doesn't call me on protesting too much. "But I do *kind of* like that Lucius Wolfe. I think he seems like he could be . . . really nice."

"I'd be lying," my dad says, instantly forgetting all about Jessup, "if I didn't admit that there's something about Lucius that scares me. There's something that's just so raw about him, like he's lived in a jungle none of the rest of us can know."

"Is that surprising?" I counter.

"No," he admits with a sad look. "No, I suppose it's not." Then he smiles, leans across the table. "I'll let you in on a little secret," he whispers. "I kind of like Lucius too. You'd think he'd be beaten down by whatever's happened to him, and yet he isn't. The boy's got spunk."

LUCIUS

Aurora may be my maybe-friend, but so far Nick Greek, Security Guard, is my only real friend here. I never seek him out, but every day when I am out in the nonsmokers' lounge he ambles over to me, strikes up a discussion.

He always asks me how school is treating me and I always say "Fine," even though it never is. I'm not much of a talker, at least not out loud, but that seems to be okay with Nick, since he *is* quite the talker.

Mostly he talks about his days playing football. I quickly get the sense that it was the best time of his life and that he anticipates none better. This makes me think about professional athletes and others who choose to let their passion be something with a predictably short shelf life, and what it must be like once their day in the sun has passed. Even if he hadn't blown out his knee, how many years would he have played total? How many before he was forced to retire and would inevitably have to face, as he does now, the rest of his life without the thing he loves to do best?

Of course, I realize he would have made a lot of money, at least, if it had worked out that way, and he wouldn't have had to resort to being a security guard at age twenty-two, so there would have been that.

Me, I know next to nothing about football, save that there is a ball involved and men running around on a large field. Sometimes it is snowing and yet still they play — I know this from watching my dad watch the games on TV. I suppose I could have asked my dad about football when I was younger, but I figured if he didn't have time to play catch with me, why should I show an interest? Now, though, since football is all that Nick ever talk-talk-talks about, I resolve that I'd better learn something about it.

Even though I don't really ever get to talk to my maybe-friend Aurora, I learn a lot by watching her. I learn a lot about friendship. For example, I see, maybe for the first time, that to have friends you have to be a friend. I start to see that the reason people gravitate so strongly to her isn't just because she's extraordinarily pretty, which she is, but rather because she listens closely to whoever is speaking to her as though she cares what he or she has to say, as though she finds the person's interests interesting.

What a concept: being interested in other people.

But now that I'm thinking maybe this is a worthwhile thing to do, and now that I'm thinking that it would be useful for talking-to-Nick purposes to know at least something about football, I take myself to the library. I would like to be able to say something more useful about the topic to him other than my usual lame, halfhearted "Go, Mets."

Tapping computer keys with hooks is not quite as challenging as jerking off with them, but it's no picnic either. I was never a great typist — only used to use about five fingers total where others would use ten, but at least it beat the peck-peck-peck of one pincer on each side.

Time to stop complaining, to stop feeling sorry for yourself and just suck it up, Lucius.

First I Google *football*.

Wow. Who would have imagined it was anything more than a bunch of big guys doing something with a funny-shaped ball on an occasionally very wet field? In fact, it turns out that football is a complex game. There are rules. There are regulations. There are plays and strategies. Really, I am beginning to think that maybe a person might need a brain to play this game. It's a little bit like chess, except people sweat a lot and there are hopefully more than just a couple figures left standing in the end.

I begin to think that maybe there are more things in life that seem simple, or even stupid, on the surface but turn out to have so much more, maybe an iceberg's ninety percent more, lurking beneath.

Funny that this is the first time this has occurred to me given that I am, well, *me*.

From simple *football* I move on to Googling *football + Nick Greek*.

Wow again. It turns out my humble pal Nick was more of a big deal than I ever would have guessed. He won all kinds of awards in high school and college, some trophy thing that sounds self-important even though I've never heard of it. I don't know much about what some of his records mean, but I do know that if he could run that many yards in so few seconds, Nick was once upon a time practically faster than a speeding bullet. And apparently some team in the NFL thought Nick was pretty impressive too, and offered him a lot of money to come play for them.

But then, before his first season started, Nick blew out his knee. Bye-bye, Nick. Bye-bye, Nick's Dream.

The whole time I've been sitting here researching, something has been percolating in my mind: it's the notion that maybe, somehow, Nick can get his dream back. Maybe he could rehabilitate that knee, get in shape again?

Every player on a football team plays a specific position with a specific title. I look to see what Nick's was.

Running back.

I shake my head. No. Whatever else Nick might ever be able to do with football, he will never be something with the word *running* in the title again.

Into the sound of the vacuum of silence created by my ceasing to tap-tap-tap on the keys, I hear a faster tap-tap-tapping.

I crane my head around the wall of my carrel to see who the fast tapper is.

It's Aurora.

I duck my head back before she sees me, stop, think.

Hey, if I'm in here researching Nick, what is she researching?

AURORA

Double amputees.

Okay, I know I told myself I wasn't going to try to discover what happened to Lucius, and I won't. I won't even add his name into the search engine here, although it would be so easy to do so. But is it so wrong to want to get more of an idea of what his life must be like? I mean, it's not exactly like I can ask him about it, and there are no other double amputees around *to* ask.

At first, what I read is the medical stuff, which is mainly disturbing, and I have to tell myself I'm reading on an intellectual level and not thinking in terms of someone I actually know.

It says that upper limb amputations are most often the result of trauma and that the amputee isn't even aware of what's been lost until waking after surgery.

I can't help it: I imagine what it must have been like for Lucius, waking up to a world in which he no longer had hands.

I shake the picture from my mind.

It talks about the rehabilitation process, not just the pain and discomfort, but the actual process of learning new strategies for things most people take for granted: eating, dressing, bathing, even going to the toilet.

But the worst is when I start reading the individual stories.

"Obviously, I can't wear a wedding ring anymore," one man writes. "My wife says she doesn't mind, that she won't wear hers either, and we can just keep the world guessing. I love that she's a good sport, but I hate the situation. I was always so proud to wear that ring. It told me who I was in the world."

"Before I lost my arms," one woman writes, "when my little girl would be upset about something, to comfort her I'd take her in my arms and stroke her hair. Well, I can still hold her well enough, but the stroking part's gone right out the window. You want to know something? It sucks. It sucks not being able to comfort your own child in the way you most want to. It sucks knowing you'll never again feel your child's cheek against your hand. Not being able to really touch other people — that's the hardest part."

"In my dreams at night," one boy writes, "I always have arms. And I can even do things in those dreams that I've never done in my life. I can throw a ball the full length of a football field. I can reach the top shelf in the kitchen without a stepstool — it's like I'm a giant too! One time, I even used my arms to fly like a bird. The worst part for me? Waking up in the morning. Every morning when I wake up, I'm surprised all over again. If I could just stay asleep for the rest of my life, I think everything would be fine."

I can't read any more of this.

I push the keyboard away as though rejecting what I've just read. It is so hard to think about this. It is so hard because I can't stop thinking about it in relation to Lucius.

Apparently I pushed the keyboard with too much force, be-cause it kicks back against the monitor, the equal and opposite reaction to that action knocking the textbook I'd left to one side to the floor.

I bend over to pick it up, fingers trembling as I grasp the hard edges of the cover.

It's when I'm down like that that I see feet beneath the carrel that's backed up against mine.

I know those feet.

They're Lucius's feet.

LUCIUS

Another two weeks pass.

I settle into my new rhythm: wake up, sit alone on bus, school, home, homework, shoot some pool, go to bed.

I have an incredibly high IQ — I've been tested — but I never got very good grades before. In my old school, I was too busy being bored or doing other stuff to get done what my parents thought I needed to get done. And as for teachers, let's just say that if I had a new upper limb for every time I heard one tell my parents "Lucius has so much potential, if only he'd apply himself," I'd have as many arms as Medusa has snakes for hair. Now, with no friends and nothing else to distract me, I get the best grades of my life.

I even find a way to work Medusa into an English essay.

My parents, at least, are pleased.

One Wednesday near the end of the school day, I see a notice pinned up outside the metal doors of the auditorium. Tryouts will be starting soon for the fall play, something called *Grease*.

Perhaps in part because I don't understand why anyone would want to write a play about grease, at first I do a homonym mixup and think it's talking about Greece the country, and I idly think my uncannily strong Medusa knowledge will come in handy here too, but then I realize my mistake.

The thumbtack is barely pushed into the wall when I see Aurora put her name up at the very top of the list.

Suddenly, being in a school play becomes the coolest thing in the world to do, and a flurry of other names go up as I watch.

Right under Aurora's goes Jessup Tristan's.

I'm shocked — I'd bet my hooks that Jessup's never tried out for a play in his life — and yet not shocked at the same time.

I think he'd do just about anything to get closer to Aurora. Hell, so would I.

Under Jessup's name goes Celia Wentworth's. Then Deanie Daily's. Then a whole slew of other names. I'm wondering, *How many roles are there in this* Grease *play? Maybe it's like* The Odyssey *or* The Iliad?

The page rapidly fills until there's just one space left. At the very bottom of the page, one final name goes up:

Lucius Wolfe.

When I get home from school, I head right out again, go to the local library, ask for a copy of *Grease.* The librarian asks me if I want the play or the movie version of the play, and I say "movie," figuring it'll be an advantage to see it. You may read a play to rehearse or memorize lines, but plays are written to be seen. Even if they're movies.

I still don't understand the implications of the title. Grease is rendered animal fat. Would you name a play *Rendered Animal Fat*? Grease is oily matter. Would you name a play *Oily Matter*? And if you want to go with the verb instead of the noun, you wind up with grease meaning "to hasten the process or progress of." Would you really want to —

You get the picture.

It's a picture that makes no sense, a picture that says "Whoever titled this play wanted to come up with the most unappetizing —"

"Just don't expect it to be exactly the same as the play," she tells me, handing me the DVD.

I study the cover. Ah! I get it now! They have grease *in their hair.*

I hand the DVD back to the librarian and wait as she runs it under the red-eyed scanner, putting a due date card in the see-through plastic pocket on the front.

"In the original, the lead female part was *not* played by an Australian," she adds, seeming very angry about this.

I wonder what she has against Australia.

Well, perhaps she was expecting Greece too.

I get the DVD home and my mom sees it before I get a chance to hide it away in my room.

"What's this?" she asks.

I know she's probably worried that I've signed out some how-to book on making a better bomb, so before she can go into full-fledged panic mode or call in the feds I show it to her.

"Oh my God!" she says, her eyes lighting up. "I saw this when it first came out! It must have been almost thirty years ago."

"It's that old, huh?"

"Watch it, buster," she says playfully, which feels good. My mom is almost never playful anymore. Then: "But why would you want to see this?"

My dad walks in as I'm answering, as I tell her that I've signed up to be in the play at school.

To her credit, my mom doesn't ask me what role I intend to try out for, but I know she must be wondering.

"You know you're not supposed to be doing any extracurriculars," my dad says gruffly, but then he takes the DVD out of Mom's hands and a slow smile spreads across his face as he looks at the woman on the cover. She's standing in the arms of what is obviously a very young John Travolta. I don't know much about popular culture, but occasionally I can't help but see the covers of magazines in drugstores and doctors' offices, so I know all about Tom Cruise, John Travolta, and Scientology. People generally seem to be worked up about this. Man, Travolta's hair looks geeky combed back like that — it's like a bad Elvis. And those eyebrows! Could he have any more makeup on them? Those eyebrows look like they were painted on with, well, a grease pencil. The woman in his arms has a skintight off-the-shoulder black top on and she's pretty hot, considering the badly teased dirty-blond hair and Vampirella eye makeup. Then, I think, maybe that's the whole point.

"Olivia Newton-John," my dad says fondly.

"Who?" Misty says, entering. She looks at the DVD cover. "Hey! I recognize her. Or at least I think I do. I think she was one of the guest judges on *American Idol* one time."

"One of your father's old crushes," Mom says.

My dad — my dad! — reddens. Then he hands the DVD back to me. "We'll all watch it together tonight," he says gruffly. "*Then* your mother and I will decide if we'll let you be in this play or not."

So that's what we do.

No sooner is dinner over than the Wolfe family kicks back in the TV room to watch the DVD of *Grease* together. Mom even makes popcorn while Dad dims the lights.

The film version of *Grease* turns out to be pretty twisted.

Even though the movie was made in the seventies, it's supposed to take place in the fifties. The action centers on a group of kids from Rydell High. The guys belong to a gang called the T-Birds and they wear black "greaser" jackets — hence the name, or maybe that refers to Travolta's hair . . . or eyebrows. The girls who hang out with the T-Birds are known as the Pink Ladies. Travolta's character's name is Danny Zuko. He's supposed to be the toughest of the tough. But when the Olivia Newton-John character, totally squeaky-clean Sandy Olsson, moves from Australia and starts going to Rydell, Danny starts to melt.

"In the original play," my dad says, "her character's name was Sandy Dumbrowski."

"Right," my mom adds. "She was never supposed to be *Australian.*"

What's with all the Australia hate everywhere all of a sudden? My dad ignores her.

It's one of those movies where everyone is always breaking into song. I guess that when I signed up for it at school I was dimly aware it was a musical, because school plays almost always are, but I don't think I realized people were still making break-into-song movies like this in the seventies.

So the basic plot is Danny likes Sandy, Sandy likes Danny, but he's a greaser while she becomes a cheerleader. People don't approve of him liking her, so he resists, and there's some other stuff with people doing outrageous things because they're jealous, particularly this one girl Rizzo — leader of the Pink Ladies — who likes Danny and is jealous of Sandy. But then Danny realizes he can't live without Sandy, he becomes a jock to win her heart, and even though his greaser friends should object to this, everyone breaks into song together in the end in one mass show of group solidarity.

Somewhere along the way, Rizzo becomes convinced she's pregnant, but then she's not.

Rama lama lama ke dinga de dinga dong.

Yeah, right.

Shoo bop shoo wadda wadda yipitty boom de boom.

I wonder how much this movie version is accurate to the play version, because it sure doesn't have a whole lot to do with reality.

"Wow," I say as the credits roll. John and Olivia are still singing. "That was deep."

"I'm still not sure we should let you do this," my dad says as Mom turns up the lights.

"It's just a play," Mom points out. I know what she's thinking. Inside, she's thinking, *Hey, at least he's not trying to join the Science Club again.*

"Yes," my dad says, "but we had an agreement. No extracurriculars."

"But it's *Grease*," my mom objects. "What kind of trouble can he get into doing *Grease*?"

"Fine," my dad says at last. Then he turns to me. "But don't louse this up. One false move, and you're out of there."

Of course, no one says that just because I'm trying out it doesn't mean I'll necessarily get the part I want. And no one dares ask just what part me and my hooks expect to get.

AURORA

The drama teacher's name is Mrs. Peepers, with oversize glasses just like that little woman in *The Incredibles,* and even I have to work not to laugh at that.

It seems that every girl who's trying out wants to be Sandy, including me. I guess it's not surprising that most people would go for the lead, but I've never been one of those people. I've always preferred seeing my name second or lower down in the program — maybe because I don't have much faith in my singing voice? — but for some reason I want this. Maybe I just don't want to be unrecognizable anymore, don't want any more little girls to mistake me for, I don't know, Toto the dog. Or maybe I'm just finally ready to take a chance on myself, ready to see if I really have what it takes.

A bunch of us girls are seated together toward the front of the auditorium, waiting our turns. The girls are supposed to all audition first, followed by the guys.

I crane my neck around and see Jessup sitting with Steve and Gary and a few others just a few rows behind us. I'm a little surprised that Jessup is even trying out. He just doesn't seem like the kind of guy who would bother acting in plays. He seems more like the kind of guy who would make fun of kids who consider themselves theater people.

Then something catches my eye even further back, far behind Jessup and the others. It's the glint of light on metal. I squint against the theater gloom, and there, all the way in the back row of the darkened auditorium, I see Lucius.

His eyes meet mine and I raise my hand, give a little wave that I hope he realizes is friendly. He raises a hook to salute me back.

"Are you sure you really want to be Sandy?" Celia whispers to me as Mrs. Peepers reads lines with one of the other girls auditioning now on the stage.

"I'm sure," I say, wondering why it should matter to her.

"But it just doesn't make any sense to me," she says, like she's annoyed. "Sandy is supposed to have blond hair. You have black hair."

"So?" I shrug. "I can wear a wig. Or maybe this time there'll just be a black-haired Sandy." I remember something. "Anything can happen. You know, in the movie version they made Sandy *Australian*."

Suddenly, I like that idea: that anything can happen.

LUCIUS

It is better to have loved and lost than to have never loved at all.

No, I know that I did not invent that line, so please do not try to sue me for plagiarism, an offense that seems to be more prevalent in our society than ever before.

But is it? Is it really better to know a thing you love only to lose it?

I think of Nick Greek and his passion for football. He got to at least have a small taste of his dream, being briefly in the NFL. Might he have been better off, though, if he'd never made it that far only to lose it, or, better yet, if he'd never had that passion to begin with? Maybe then he would have applied himself to more practical things while in school. Maybe there would have been more options available to him now. Maybe he would have been happier.

And what of me and my hands? Or, I should say, lack of hands.

My parents have an unusual preference for the musical sound of blind singers. Ray Charles, Stevie Wonder, Andrea Bocelli — they have them all. What of those men and their blindness? People always regard them as men who have overcome so much, and yet I cannot see it that way, no pun intended. Having sight and then losing it, knowing all the colors of the world only to have them disappear — that is a tragedy. But you don't mourn what you have never known. Indeed, it is the only existence you *do* know.

I often think, far too often, that I would have been better off had I been born the way I am now. Sometimes it is agony to think of all the things my hands once did, now can no longer do, will never do again.

If I'd known then what I know now . . .

But that's always the thing, isn't it? When you're living a thing — like Nick living football or me living hands — you *don't* know. You take it for granted, like a dog being petted, assuming it will somehow go on forever.

If I'd known then what I know now . . .

I'd have touched everything in sight, everything I could get my hands on. I'd have grabbed the nearest girl I could find and, not even caring how crazy she thought me, touched my hands to her face just to know what that feels like.

Is it better to have loved and lost than to have never loved at all?

I, never having loved before, have no real answer to that question.

———

I can't say I'm surprised that Aurora has the voice of an angel when she sings.

It's a good thing I don't have hands anymore, I think, because if I did, I'd be clapping to the point of embarrassing myself.

One good thing, I quickly note, as I listen to the others read their lines onstage while I follow along with the copy of the script Mrs. Peepers gave me: the play version of *Grease* takes place in Chicago, which I find to be a more apt setting than the beachy California look of the film. One bad thing: the name of the guys' gang is the Burger Palace Boys, not the T-Birds. I don't know — Burger Palace Boys sounds like a lame name to me for a tough gang.

I'm listening to Celia sing — she's actually not half bad, but totally wrong for Sandy; she's a deep alto — when in my peripheral vision I catch sight of a shadow in the row I'm seated in, snaking its way toward me.

"Hooks!" I hear Jessup greet me as he, uninvited, parks his butt in the seat next to mine. He says his nickname for me in an overly cheerful way, as though I could somehow mistake us for friends.

I ignore him.

"So, Hooks," he says, still trying. "What part are you trying out for? I hear they had an Australian Sandy in the movie, but I don't think anyone's ever played any of these roles with hooks before. Are you hoping to be the first disabled Danny?"

I have no doubt he is pleased with his alliteration: "disabled Danny." I suppose I could counter with my own alliteration by saying, "Are you hoping to be the first dickhead Danny?"

But I don't say that. I don't say anything, don't tell him that I can't sing to save my life and that he has nothing to worry about in that regard.

Instead, I keep my eyes on the stage.

"Come on, Hooks. Who are you going to be? Johnny Casino, the rock-star wannabe? Vince Fontaine, the slimy disc jockey?

Eugene Florczyk, the *nerd?*" His eyes brighten. "I know!" He does a remarkably good falsetto. "You're going to be Teen Angel, right? You could play it no-armed. Sounds sick to me, but who ever knows what chicks will go for? Maybe you'd even wind up with groupies." Then in a normal voice: "C'mon, Hooks — tell me."

I let him wait another moment, then answer:

"Wouldn't you like to know."

AURORA

I must admit: I am shocked at what a good singer Jessup is. In fact, he is so far and away better than any of the other guys, it's impossible to think Mrs. Peepers will give the role to anyone *but* him.

And I see what's coming when Mrs. Peepers asks Jessup and me to go back up onstage at the same time, instructing us to sing a few stanzas of "Summer Nights," the first duet that Danny and Sandy have together.

I can't lie: Jessup and I sound good together and I feel the excitement in the room. The play calls for me to look at him intensely and I do that, startled at how intensely he looks back. There's something naked and disturbing, and yet somehow compelling in his steady gaze. It doesn't necessarily compel me, but I can see where other girls would find it so, find it impossible to tear away, find it impossible not to give in. It's a curious thing, becoming aware of how much a guy wants you. And yet, while all this is going on, I am constantly aware of Lucius's presence at the back of the room.

Jessup and I are the only ones Mrs. Peepers has do this — sing together to see how our duet sounds — so everyone else can't help but know what's coming too.

"I can't believe this," Celia mutters at my side as we wait outside afterward for Mrs. Peepers to post the names of the cast on the auditorium door. "Sandy is supposed to be a blonde, not dark."

I'm tempted to point out that as a redhead, she's no closer to Sandy's true hair color than I am, and that if Mrs. Peepers just wants a blonde, then she might as well choose Deanie, whose singing, I'm sorry to say, is just plain awful. But I keep my mouth shut, sensing that this dose of common sense will not go over well at this moment.

So instead I simply wait with the others.

LUCIUS

"You're a redhead," I whisper into Celia Wentworth's ear.

She blinks as she turns to face me. This is the first time, outside of Aurora and Nick, that I've spoken to anyone without having them speak to me first, and she's shocked, as if I've struck her or something.

"What's that supposed to mean?" she says.

"Just that if hair color were the sole barometer for the suitability for the part, and not talent, you'd be just as far out of the running as you seem to think Aurora should be."

Many people have looked at me with disgust or revulsion since I started at this school, and some — I'm thinking specifically of Jessup here — regularly look at me with contempt. But no one so far, at least not that I've seen, has looked at me with the naked hatred that Celia Wentworth is bestowing on me right now.

Before she has a chance to respond, however, Mrs. Peepers emerges, tacks the cast list to the door, and then silently but hurriedly departs down the hall, as though someone might physically tackle her for her casting decisions.

The cast list has no surprises at the top.

Aurora Belle is to play Sandy Dumbrowski, which is perfect, Aurora as heroine.

Jessup Tristan is to play Danny Zuko. I can't help but feel a sigh of disappointment escape me here as I stand at the back of the group. Jessup is not, nor will he ever be, a hero; not even an antihero — that would be me. Really, I'd like to tackle Mrs. Peepers to the ground now myself, or at least beg her to let someone, anyone else, play opposite Aurora.

Most of the rest of the casting is inconsequential, as far as I'm concerned.

Celia Wentworth as the morally questionable Rizzo, a role I think will suit her; Steve, the boy I've come to think of as Steve-with-No-Last-Name, as Kenickie, arguably the stupidest and nerdiest name of any character in any play ever. Deanie Daily will be Frenchy; Gary Addams will be Doody, which, come to think of it, rivals Kenickie for worst name ever.

And there are others, going down the list in descending importance.

I feel many pairs of eyes swivel back to look at me when they reach the last line on the list. Most of the eyes are hostile, except for one pair. Those eyes are surprised, happy at what they've seen. They are Aurora's eyes.

And what have they all seen?

That on the very last line, it reads:

Lucius Wolfe, Stage Manager

This time, I didn't even have to use the words "discrimination" or "lawsuit." I didn't even have to pull out the old trusty "My civil rights are being violated here."

It's amazing how easy it is to get something no one else wants.

AURORA

We settle in to a routine of practicing Mondays through Thursdays after school.

At first, a lot of the other cast and stage crew are resistant to the idea of Lucius being stage manager. It's like they think someone with hooks for hands can't fulfill this important role, but all their talking about it just makes me think they've never been in a real play before.

The stage manager in any theatrical production acts as an almost equal to the assistant director during rehearsals. The stage manager, in this case Lucius, keeps all the technical information on cues and blocking and necessary props and everything else.

When opening night comes, he essentially takes control of running the show. He calls the cues for all transitions while also functioning as Communications Central for the cast and crew. Without him, the actors would be singing in the dark or the curtain would rise to an empty stage.

It's a massive job for one person, and it also makes me wonder why the director is billed far above the stage manager in playbills. I mean, really: What *does* Mrs. Peepers do all day? What is Mrs. Peepers doing while Lucius does all of this?

And yet he does it all, quietly and without complaint, and before too many days go by, the other cast members have to accept that Lucius is doing a phenomenal job and is here to stay. They don't even snicker at him anymore when he occasionally loses control of the pencil he holds in his pincers.

One nice thing about playing the Wicked Witch of the West, like I did back in my old school? You're not expected to kiss anybody.

Since this is just a high school production, Jessup and I aren't expected to have as much physical contact as the characters in the original play do, but we *are* expected to kiss at the end.

"Um," I say to Mrs. Peepers, "do we really need to rehearse this part? I mean, everyone knows how to kiss. It's not like one of the complicated dance numbers or something. So maybe we could just save it for the night of the actual performance?"

Jessup, who has surprised me by being very professional and even kind during our rehearsals, bends over to whisper in my ear, "What's wrong, Aurora? Haven't you ever been kissed before?"

"Of course I have," I say, feeling the blush redden my cheeks, but I am lying. In truth, I have never kissed any boy before, not on the lips. I know that most girls my age already have, and more, but there wasn't a whole lot of time for me to start kissing boys, what with my mom dying and all. And since then? I've been too busy worrying about my dad. Plus, there haven't been any boys I've wanted to kiss before. Okay, so maybe I am an odd girl. But it's better than doing things with guys just for the sake of doing them or, worse, saying yes to anything for fear of being laughed at when in reality you want to say no.

But if you're an actress, you can't say no to a kiss, not when it's scripted. So my objections fall on deaf Mrs. Peepers ears and she insists that Jessup and I perform the final scene as Jacobs and Casey wrote it. It makes me think immediately that my dad is wrong after all: that sometimes writers insert things that shouldn't be played out literally as written.

When the moment comes for Jessup-as-Danny to kiss me, he takes his time, placing both his hands on the sides of my face before slowly lowering his face to mine.

His lips at last touch my lips.

I'm pretty sure that a high school play is not supposed to have a kiss go on for this long, no matter how it is written in the script. I feel Jessup-as-Danny's lips press more firmly into mine before finally, at last, he pulls away.

"There," he whispers, keeping his voice even lower than a stage whisper so no one else can hear. "That wasn't so bad, was it?"

"No," I say, lying, while inside I am thinking: *I just had my first kiss.*

And it was nothing like I'd ever dreamed it would be.

Then I tell myself that it is just a play, that it is just rehearsal, and that it doesn't count.

LUCIUS

I have to admit: standing here and watching Jessup kiss Aurora, and being powerless to do anything to stop it, ranks right up there with some of the worst things that have happened to me.

But I also have to admit, they look like they belong together: two beautiful people kissing.

And one last thing I have to admit: I've been keeping a close eye on Jessup these past several days, and what I've seen has made me wonder if I could be wrong about him. He's taking his acting very seriously and I've noticed he's very attentive to Aurora, doing his best to make sure she's shown off to best advantage in the scenes that they share together, that she's comfortable. It's almost as though he's a character from a fairy tale, Prince Charming, the guy who's always willing to just look like a neutered Ken doll so that the Barbie beside him can shine that much more brightly. And Aurora mostly looks happy when she's onstage with him, making me wonder if maybe it might not be bad for her to wind up with someone like him. After all, like her, he's got everything.

Jessup has even been nice to me lately, at least whenever Aurora's around. Every day now, he invites me to eat lunch with them. But every day I decline. I've gotten used to eating by myself.

But even though I'm starting to think Jessup might not be half bad, even though I'm starting to think that maybe he and

Aurora belong together, seeing them kiss onstage is just too much to bear.

So I busy myself with working on my bible for the play, with making sure all the props get returned to their appropriate places as rehearsal ends.

The only problem is, I'm so busy keeping myself busy, I miss my bus.

What am I going to do now? I wonder, as I race after the bus, miss it as it pulls out of the parking lot. Who would have ever thought I'd wish to be on a bus?

"What's wrong, Lucius?" a sweet voice behind me asks.

I turn to see Aurora standing there. Beside her is her father, the librarian, Mr. Belle. Every time I see him, I always like Mr. Belle. It's not as though we have these great conversations — we don't — it's more that, unlike all the other teachers and administrators in this school, he always looks at me like I could be just any normal kid and not maybe a disaster waiting to happen. You've gotta love a guy who sees the good in all people, even if you never see that yourself.

"That was my bus." I can't prevent a groan, almost a whine, from entering my voice. "I'm supposed to take the late bus home from rehearsal," I say, "and that was the last bus. My parents are going to kill me if I'm not home on time."

"No worries," Mr. Belle says easily. "We'll be happy to give you a lift. Why, with all the stops the bus has to make, we'll probably even get you home early."

"Thanks," I say, climbing into the back of their Volvo. I'm uncomfortable having people do stuff for me out of pity, but I see no way around it: my parents weren't crazy about my working on the play in the first place, and I'm worried that if I'm late, even once, they'll change their minds.

I have so little life outside my home, even in my home, I have so little that's mine, it would be death to have that little taken away.

As we drive, I talk only when I need to tell Mr. Belle what streets to turn at; apparently, he knows this town as poorly as I do. So, since I'm not talking, I sit back and listen to the pleasant sound of Mr. Belle and Aurora's chatter swirling around me. Mr. Belle asks Aurora how the play is going and she explains in detail, filling him in that I'm the stage manager. Their voices are so happy, the questions they ask each other so innocent — as though neither is suspecting the other of harboring anything dark. It's so different from the way my own family sounds, I could almost resent it. And yet, I don't. I'm just glad for Aurora, that she has this happy world. She deserves it.

"So, how about it, Lucius?" Mr. Belle's words break through my thoughts.

"Excuse me, sir?" I say.

"Daddy just asked you if you'd like to have dinner with us tonight," Aurora says.

"But we're almost at my house," I say, feeling an unreasonable panic begin to well up inside. Funny how you can hate a place and yet have an unreasonable need for it. I wonder if this is what convicts feel like, hating prison and yet somehow acting in ways that land them back there again and again.

"But you can still call your parents and ask them, can't you?" Mr. Belle counters amiably. Really, was there ever such an amiable man as Mr. Belle?

In a way, his amiability right now is downright annoying. Still, there's no need to let him suspect this, certainly no need to let him think my life is anything other than normal, so I attempt to paint my parents as strict as opposed to pathologically worried about what I might do if left on my own for too long.

"I'm not sure my parents would like that, sir," I say. "They're pretty strict about me staying in on, um, school nights." That's good, I think: a parent/librarian should appreciate other parents being serious about their dedication to their children's studies as opposed to this lax attitude you see everywhere these days. There's no need, I think, to tell Mr. Belle that except for school activities and the occasional trip to the library, I'm really not allowed out of the house on my own.

Mr. Belle's eyes meet mine in the rearview mirror. I can tell he knows there's something not quite right here, but it's impossible to read what he's thinking.

I make sure to keep my own expression vacantly innocent as I hold his penetrating gaze. Are my eyes open wide enough? Yes, I think they must be, because my eyeballs are starting to hurt from all the air hitting against them.

"Fine," he finally says. "Then I'll ask your parents for you. Now, then, how do we get the rest of the way to your house?"

Oh, great. This should really be good.

When we pull in to the driveway, Mr. Belle tells Aurora and me to stay in the car. It's late afternoon now, almost early evening, but the day has been warm so the car windows are all half open, hence all the air on my overexposed eyeballs. The half-open windows mean that Aurora and I can hear the sound of Mr.

Belle's soles clacking along the pavement, hear the sound of him knocking at the door.

We hear when my mother answers, "Yes?" as she opens the door.

We hear Mr. Belle's voice, sounding as though if he had a hat on his head he would raise it in polite greeting now, say, "I'm Robert Belle, Mrs. Wolfe. I'm the librarian at your son's school."

We hear as my mother, a mixture of horror and worry in her voice, groans, "Oh, no. What has Lucius done now?"

The shocked tone of Mr. Belle's voice when he responds makes me immediately aware that in his world — in Aurora's world — parents don't automatically assume the worst of their children.

"Oh, no!" Mr. Belle says. "It's nothing like that! It's just that your son is stage managing the play my daughter is in, I offered to give him a lift home" — I notice, gratefully, that Mr. Belle artfully avoids telling my mom I missed the bus, as though he knows instinctively this will make her hostile to his request — "and when we were almost here, it occurred to me how pleasant it would be to have him join us for dinner this evening."

Again, I am sure that if Mr. Belle were wearing a hat, he would politely doff it at my mom now.

I am positive that I have never in my life seen my mom simper before, and yet, as I cautiously peek out the window, I note that she is practically doing so now.

"Well, if you really want him, Mr. Belle . . ." Is my mother *blushing*?

"Oh, we do, Mrs. Wolfe, we really do," he reassures her.

"I guess that'll be okay, then," she says. Then she sterns up, as though she's just reminded herself that she's supposed to be a parent and not a pushover; a parent of a boy like me, no less. "But don't keep him out too late," she warns.

"I wouldn't dream of it, Mrs. Wolfe," he says with one last invisible hat doff.

A minute later, I raise my hook to wave goodbye to my mom as we drive away in the car.

I can't believe it. For the first time in forever, I'm going to eat dinner with someone other than my family.

I hope I don't spill things all over myself.

The house Aurora and her father live in is so different from my own house, I immediately feel as though I'm stepping into another world.

It's tough to put my finger — if I still had one — on what exactly it is, but there's just a generous warmth that permeates everything here. Even though my family's lived in the new house for a few months, it's still as though we just moved in yesterday, as though we might be moving out again at any moment. But here, well, it feels as though the people residing under this roof actually *live* here. Even the smallest items have a wanted and loved look about them, not at all like the things people buy just to have something serviceable.

"Can I get you something to drink while I get supper ready?" Mr. Belle offers. "Lemonade? Soda?"

"Water will be fine, thank you," I say, not sure what to do with my hooks, I'm feeling so awkward — when I try to cross them casually across my chest as I've seen other guys do, my hooks protrude alarmingly — so I just put my arms crossed at the wrist behind my back. "I'm not much of one for soda."

"You're my new hero," Mr. Belle says. "I'll buy you a car if you can convert my daughter to your way of thinking."

"Dad!" When Aurora says it, she turns it into two syllables, accompanying the word with such a dramatic eye roll, if we were in the auditorium at school ticket holders in the back row could still see it. But I can tell she's not really bothered. She doesn't mind her dad's teasing.

"Can I help with anything?" I offer as Mr. Belle removes items from the fridge: chicken breasts, the fixings for a salad, corn on the cob.

"Nope," Mr. Belle says. "I've got it all under control."

I thank the gods he doesn't ask me to shuck the corn for him. Who knows what sort of mess I'd make out of *that* simple chore.

As I'm breathing my sigh of relief, Mr. Belle reaches into a cabinet down next to the sink and pulls out a frilly-edged apron that he proceeds to put on over his shirt and tie. I'm not accustomed to laughing at other people, but it does look funny. I make eye contact with Aurora and ask a question with my raised eyebrows, but she just shrugs, rolls her eyes again.

"Where's Mrs. Belle?" I think to ask. I'm a guest in someone else's home, I remind myself, for the first time in a very long time. I should do my best to be a good guest, to show interest in their lives. Isn't that what a normal person would do? "Does she work late usually?"

Mr. Belle's back is to me as he answers. He's chopping a tomato and he doesn't stop. "Mrs. Belle is no more, I'm afraid."

It takes me a while to process this, and then . . .

Ouch. I've really put my foot in it this time, I think, based on the sudden ramrod look of Mr. Belle's back. I figure he must be divorced, and recently so.

"My mother's dead," Aurora adds. "She died a few months ago."

More processing.

The enormity of what they've just shared with me — I feel as though I've just taken a punch to the gut. And for the first time, maybe ever, I realize that there are worse things than losing your hands.

"I'm sorry," I say lamely. "I wouldn't have said anything. I didn't know."

"It's okay, son," Mr. Belle says, his back still to me as he goes to work on a head of lettuce; it's funny, I don't think my own father has ever called me "son," and yet this man does it so easily the very first time I am in his house.

I recognize the green stuff in his hands as romaine lettuce and I think, inanely, how all my mom ever buys is iceberg.

"There's no reason you should have," Mr. Belle goes on. "After all, it's not like people go through their lives with signs on their foreheads saying 'This is the awful thing that happened to me this year.'"

Actually, it's funny he should say that, since my hooks are my own constant testament to "This is the awful thing that happened to me last year."

"I really am sorry," I say to Aurora. *Sorry* — I know it's inadequate to what they've been through, but it's all that I've got.

"It's okay, Lucius," Aurora says.

Since there's no way to make this moment better, and no way I can take back the last pain-filled moment or the last period of however long these two have been hurting, I simply say, "If you show me where you keep the plates and things, I can set the table for you."

And I do, taking great care not to drop anything or make a disturbing sound.

After dinner, a surprisingly jovial meal given what has gone before, Mr. Belle says he has some work to do in his office.

"Why don't you and Aurora take dessert out on the patio?" he offers. "I promise I'll still get you home at a reasonable hour like I told your mother I would."

So we take our plates with slices of lemon meringue pie out onto the patio.

The evening is starting to get cool out here, the glow of the early moon making the light from the colored lanterns behind us unnecessary. As I fork up some of the unnaturally yellow filling and lightly toasted meringue of the pie, careful as I was all during supper not to make a visible slob of myself, I think how at my house we never sit outside in the evening, or any time really. We are always inside, inside, hiding away from the world.

"What happened to your mom?" I ask into the silence.

It is a somewhat rude question, I realize as soon as I ask it. And yet now that I have been informed of Mrs. Belle's death, it somehow feels as though I would be even ruder not to ask it, as though I was willfully ignoring the eight-hundred-pound gorilla in the room.

"She got sick," Aurora says, an obvious sadness tingeing her tone as she answers straightforwardly. "She got sick with cancer several years ago. Then she got sicker and sicker. And then she died."

It is a story without details. And yet, I wonder, what details does it need? It is all there, in the four short sentences she has spoken: an impossible sorrow, a world of pain.

I lay down my fork, carefully place my plate on the little redwood table that attaches the two chairs we are sitting in. I think how Mr. Belle and Aurora probably sit out here often in the evenings. As we move further into fall and then winter, they will probably stop.

I wipe my mouth with the napkin, fold it, and place it across the top of the empty plate.

"I'm sorry," I say again.

"I know," she says. Then:

"What happened to your hands?" she asks softly, at last unable to ignore the other eight-hundred-pound gorilla.

Really, between the two of us, we are practically a zoo out here.

No one has ever asked me this question before, unless you count Nick Greek, and for some reason I don't count him right now. I suppose I always knew this day would come, but I also always assumed I would simply answer "None of your business." And yet now that the moment is here, and I see the sincere concern in Aurora's eyes, I can't help but tell her the story.

I study the trees, punctuating what I assume must be the far edge of their property. In a knothole in one of the trees, a squirrel is busy with some kind of squirrel-type industry. I study the trees a moment longer, and then I start to speak.

"I stole some chemicals from the science lab at my old school," I say, not meeting her eyes, still looking at the tree line. But out of the corner of my eye I see that she's not looking at me either. She too is staring straight ahead. I have an impulse, an almost hysterical impulse to laugh that right now it is like we are two people sharing the same bad roller-coaster ride at a beat-up old amusement park. I control the impulse.

"What kind of chemicals?" she asks.

"Sodium, magnesium — the authorities said afterward they found traces of eight others." Now that I've started, I'm ready to tell it all, and I do so, not waiting for her to prompt me along with any more questions.

"The school claimed afterward that they had no idea how I'd stolen them. They claimed they took every precaution to keep them safe. But, apparently" — I allow myself a wry grin — "they didn't really take *every* precaution. It was a day when we didn't have any school, but it wasn't a regular vacation. You know? It was like one of those crazy days we get off every now and then: Teacher Redevelopment Day or something like that. I had the chemicals down in the basement of our old house — I had my own little lab set up down there, on the other side of the room from our old pool table — and I was trying to . . . *make* something. But, I don't know, something didn't go the way it was supposed to, and there was this explosion." I take a breath, release it.

"It was an accident. My dad was at work and I thought my mom and little sister were out shopping. But it turns out, as I discovered after I regained consciousness, they weren't. They were in a room at the other side of the house and, thank God, neither of them was hurt."

"But you were," she puts in softly.

"I was," I answer steadily, not feeling sorry for myself at all. "I blew off my hands. My chest and stomach? You do *not* want to see that." I think how at that first gym class Jessup called me Frankenstein, and for some reason I almost smile in the half-dark. "I don't know why my face wasn't damaged beyond repair. I guess the universe decided to spare me just one piece of luck that day — well, three, including my mom and sister being okay. But I was in critical condition for a long time, spent a month in an oxygen tent. And our old house? The assessment put the damages at being almost what my parents had spent on the house ten years earlier. I used to wonder, after I got out of the oxygen tent: How is it possible for damages to almost equal worth?" I shake my head. "I don't think my parents have ever forgiven me, my sister neither."

The recitation of my tale is far longer than what she said about the loss of her mother, and yet Aurora's reaction is an exact replica of mine, perhaps because some stories don't allow for a lengthy response.

"I'm sorry," she says.

"I know," I say, well versed in my lines and content to speak them.

I do note that she doesn't ask me the one thing I think nearly every other person would ask me right now: Just what exactly was

I trying to . . . *make* with those ten chemicals? — and I am grateful for this. Somehow, I sense that it is not a lack of curiosity or imagination; it is respect. And again I am grateful.

One thing she can't possibly know: I've left one crucial fact out of the telling.

"So," Aurora asks, shifting gears completely, just as I did earlier in their kitchen after Aurora told me her mother had died, "are you going to Jessup's party a week from Friday?"

"I haven't heard anything about any party," I say, which is a lie. All week long, it's been impossible to avoid hearing Jessup invite kids all around me.

Aurora's pretty brow furrows in puzzlement. "That's funny," she says. "It's supposed to be for the entire cast and crew. Jessup said so."

I shrug, pretend I don't care. "I must not be invited," I say.

"But that's impossible," she says. "It's supposed to be for everyone involved with the play." She laughs, a wind-chime sound, as she adds, "Well, except for Mrs. Peepers." Then quick, before I realize what she's doing, she reaches out a hand and places it on my arm, not the plastic of my lower arm — no, not that — on my upper arm, where there is real skin beneath my shirt.

I feel as though my whole body could explode at her touch. Nobody ever touches me if it can be avoided. And, for the most part, I have been content to keep the world at this distance; at arm's length, if you will. But not now. This is the first time that anyone outside of my family has touched me in a very long time, and my entire body feels it, enjoys it, fears it.

"Please come, Lucius," she says, as if it really does matter to her: whether I'm at Jessup's party or not.

I look at her: that dark-angel hair, those serene-ocean eyes. She is, I think, the most beautiful girl I have ever seen. And yet somehow, that doesn't matter in the slightest. She could lose that physical beauty tomorrow and she would still be Aurora. Everything is who she is, *what* she is.

"Please," she says again. "You deserve to have some fun. We both do."

Gently, so as not to scare her, I extract my arm from her touch. I can't bear to be touched by her any more because despite her intensity, I know she cannot possibly like me *in that way*, as people say.

Still, how can I say no to her?

AURORA

Well, of *course* I want to know. But he didn't offer and I didn't ask:

What was he trying to make with all those chemicals?

LUCIUS

"So how's work on the play coming?" Nick Greek asks. "You enjoying it?"

"Yes," I say, an automatic answer, just like saying "fine" whenever he asks me how school is going. But as soon as the word is out of my mouth, I realize it's true: I *am* enjoying myself.

It gives me a new and rare feeling of competence, stage managing the play so well, even if it is just, you know, *Grease*.

But I can't say that out loud to Nick — there would be an implied admission that so much of the time I *don't* feel competent, not as a student in this school, not as anything else on this planet — so I seek to change the subject.

Besides, there's something I've been percolating in my mind ever since I did research on Nick and football. And I've done yet more research on football since then. I've been growing an idea in my mind.

I open my mouth to speak, shut it again.

Do I really want to do this? For if I do, and if my idea is a success, it could ultimately take Nick away from me, and he's the only person who has real conversations with me every day.

Then I decide I *do* want to do it. If he is my friend, and I believe he is, and if friendship means wanting what's best for the other person and not simply what's best for the other person in relation to you, then I *have* to do it. I am ethically bound.

"Have you ever thought," I pose the question cautiously, "about doing something in football besides being a running back?"

Nick snorts. "What do you mean? Like being the water boy?"

"Nothing like that," I say. And then I snort back for emphasis, just to show we're on the same page. "But isn't there, oh, I don't know, *some* position, some *playing* position on a football team that doesn't involve needing to run much?"

It takes a moment, a long moment, but then a light dawns in Nick's eyes.

And that's how it starts.

"I never thought about being a kicker before," Nick says. "I never *wanted* to be a kicker before."

"Yeah?" I say, my breath fogging the air as I speak the word. "Well, I never wanted to be without hands either. C'mon, let's go."

The mornings have turned cool as we've moved further into fall, meaning early mornings are a real bitch. I swear, if I still had hands, I'd need to blow on them right now to keep them warm. Still, I am happy to be out here on this football field, two hours before school starts.

It has been my master plan.

When I asked Nick if there was a position in football that didn't require running, he answered what my research had already taught me: kicker.

"But I can't run much anymore," Nick said, "and I certainly can't run well."

"But you can run ten feet, can't you?" I said.

"I guess."

"Well, that's all you need. No one expects speed from a kicker. And kickers are always in demand in the NFL, I know I read that somewhere," I said, warming to my subject. "Kickers run hot and cold. Last year's great kicker can be this year's goat."

Nick's eyes narrowed.

"Why are you reading up on football?" he asked.

"I'm a polymath." I shrugged.

Nick looked at me like I was talking Greek.

"A person who knows a little bit about everything," I explained, "kind of like a walking encyclopedia." I shrugged again. Suddenly I was shrug-happy. "I just like knowing things, I guess."

And that's how we end up out on a frosty playing field at the dawn of the morning. Well, first I had to talk my parents into letting me drive to school with Nick in the mornings, but that turned out to be easier than expected. Apparently, once my mother caved to my going somewhere in Mr. Belle's car, it suddenly became okay for me to go anywhere so long as a school authority was driving me. And my dad was particularly tickled that what I wanted to do had something to do with sports, but I refused to go into specifics with him.

Nick does some warming-up exercises that look funny to me, but I have to assume he knows what he's doing.

When he says he's finally ready, I become his holder. If this were a real football game, I'd be catching the snap from the center before holding the ball in place so that Nick could try to kick it through the goalposts for a field goal. But this isn't a real football game: there's just the two of us, and I'm all Nick's got.

We're each all the other's got.

I let him set the pace in the beginning. The first kick Nick takes is from fifteen yards from the goal line. He comes at the ball kind of slow, and when he gets close to it, he nails it at an angle with the foot on his good leg. It sails right through.

It doesn't sail through every time.

But we keep practicing.

As the sky slowly brightens, I gradually move the ball farther and farther from those goalposts. I think of what a funny thing it is: the farther the goal, the more impressive.

I move the ball to the twenty-five-yard line, the thirty-five, the forty-five.

I don't usually talk a lot, but as Nick practices, I become a regular chatterbox.

"Did you know," I say, "that Tom Dempsey holds the record for the longest field goal ever?"

Nick just grunts as he kicks at the ball again, this time from the fifty-five-yard line. I must say, I'm awfully glad he hasn't kicked my hooks off yet.

"And did you know," I say, "that he scored that field goal — sixty-three yards! — in a game between New Orleans and Detroit?"

Nick grunts again. Sixty yards now.

As I say, Nick doesn't sail it through every time, but he does so often enough. And when he misses, it's always close. The man is a natural athlete. He must've been something else when he could still run.

In addition to blind singers, my parents have a thing for musicians who died in the sixties, whether singers or not. So they like

Jimi Hendrix and Janis Joplin and they also like an early Rolling Stone who died in a swimming pool, Brian Jones. They always say he was the best Stone, that the band was never the same after he died, that he was a musician's musician who could pick up a new instrument in the morning and have it mastered by sunset.

It seems to me that Nick is like that with sports.

I sure hope Nick doesn't end up dead in a swimming pool.

"And did you know," I say, from the sixty-three-yard line now, "that that record has stood since November 8, 1970? Most good kickers can only kick fifty-five yards . . . tops! No one has been able to beat that sixty-three-yard record in —"

"Give it a rest, kid," Nick says. "I'm not going to beat Dempsey's record today. You've really gotta stop with all that polymath stuff. Your head will explode."

"Yeah, but did you also know that Dempsey set the record *kicking with just half a foot?*"

"Actually," Nick says, "I did know that."

Even though he hasn't done any running, Nick is winded now. I guess all that kicking must take a lot out of a person.

"You're good at this," I tell him as he stands there, bent over at the waist, hands resting against slightly bent knees.

"Yeah, but it's not running," he says.

"Nothing ever will be again," I say, recognizing the need to be honest. "But so what? It's still football. It can still get you back on that field again."

This is, I think, what it must mean to be human: to want something good for someone else.

So that's what we do in the mornings out there on the playing field: we chase after the remainder of a dream.

During those mornings, I think of my own compromised dreams, my own situation: I'd love to be able to touch Aurora with the hands I used to have, but I'd give anything just to touch her at all.

AURORA

"Have you noticed how much time that Lucius guy spends with that security guard?" Deanie Daily asks me.

"Jessup says they even do stuff out on the playing fields in the mornings before school starts," Celia Wentworth adds. "What's up with that? I think maybe Mr. Hooks is *gay*."

"Shut up, Celia," I say without thinking about it first. "And so what if he is?"

LUCIUS

The first hurdle to getting to Jessup's party is getting my parents to let me go to the party.

As expected, there is resistance.

"I don't think this is such a good idea," my mom says.

"I *know* this isn't a good idea," my dad says.

"Well, *I* think this is an *excellent* idea," Misty says.

What's going on? Since when is my little sister my biggest champion?

"You *do?*" my mom and dad and I all say to Misty at the same time.

"Of course," Misty says, as though it must be obvious to one and all. "Lucius can't spend his whole life in this house, can he?"

"I don't know," my dad says. "Can't he?"

"Dad," Misty says.

"Sorry." My dad holds his hands up. "It was just a joke."

"He does have the play," my mom points out. "He gets out of the house for that. Plus the time he spends playing football in the morning with that security guard."

"And that's good," Misty says, "but it's not enough. Lucius needs to start living a normal life again. How can he ever be normal if he doesn't?"

You would think my parents would have a whole list of arguments for this — and I myself, if it weren't counterproductive to my goals, would just love to ask Misty to define *normal* or, better yet, tell us all why it is such a wonderful thing to be — but they surprise us, surprise even themselves, by caving to Misty's greater wisdom on the subject of what kids need.

"Fine," my dad relents. "But your mom will drop you off when the party starts, I'll pick you up at eleven, and if I hear any reports of you misbehaving, this will be the last party you go to until you turn fifty."

"Fine," I agree to everything. Really, if they held a contract out to me right now, I would sign it.

But then, no sooner do I feel elation about going to the party — I, Lucius Wolfe, am going to a party! — than deflation sets in as I am faced with an unimaginable horror: *What am I going to wear?*

Ever since the explosion, my mom has gone out by herself to buy my clothes. And before that? Well, fashion wasn't big on my mind back then — I was more into chemicals — so whatever I wore, Mom bought those things too. And it's not like anything she's ever bought has been really awful: no red plaid short-sleeved cotton shirts with one pocket at the chest, perfect for holding pocket protectors and a load of leaky pens; no polyester pants that hike up so high the belt fits under my neck, perfect for hanging myself because I look so geeky in the neck-high pants. But I know the clothes I wear are not quite the same as the clothes worn by the other guys at school, at least not the cool guys. Like I say, there's nothing distinctly *wrong* about what I wear, but there's nothing particularly right about it either. It's like everything I own is just a little bit off.

So what do I do?

I go to the best fashion consultant I know.

"Misty?" I knock on my kid sister's door Saturday morning.

Misty may be three years younger than I am, but I know she is already crushing on guys my age and that she pays a lot of attention to what everyone wears. She reads fashion magazines as though they were important books, and if there is a trend blowing in on the next wind, Misty will catch hold of it before any of her friends do. In fact, she's reading a fashion magazine when I knock, lying on her stomach diagonally across her bed, headphones clapped down over her ears.

I approach the bed, hook one of the earphones away from her ear so I can say, "Misty?" again, louder this time.

She gives a little jump, flipping over on her side.

"Lucius." She puts her hand to her chest. "You scared me."

"Sorry," I say, "but . . ." *Man,* this is suddenly awkward. "I need your help." I shuffle my feet, stare down at them. Should I wash my sneakers? "I don't know what to wear to the party next Friday."

She stares at me in stunned silence. Then a look of mild disgust takes over her face. "God, you people are hopeless. How did I end up in such a family?"

She doesn't wait for an answer as she rolls off the bed. "I'll tell you one thing," she says, "you're not going to find whatever you need in that closet of yours." She grabs on to one of my hooks, a thing she's never done before. "Come on," she says. "Let's go find Mom."

Oh, brother, I think.

———◆———

We find Mom folding towels in the laundry room.

"Mom," Misty says authoritatively, "Lucius and I need you to drive us to the mall. If Lucius is going to this party, he's going to need some new clothes."

My mom looks at me and then turns back to Misty. It's as though I'm a character on TV they're critiquing, as though they don't realize I can hear them.

"What's wrong with what he has on?" my mom asks.

"Are you *kidding* me?" Misty sounds disgusted.

I look down at what I'm wearing. So, okay. So maybe I'm not going to be asked to front for a boy band, and I know I already dissed my own wardrobe, but I don't think I look *that* bad . . .

"Everything's wrong with it," Misty informs my mom. "That shirt? Those jeans? Those *sneakers?*" Misty looks like she's getting a headache just thinking about it. "He can't go to a party in clothes like that."

"Well, I still don't see —" Mom starts to object.

"No, he really can't," Misty cuts her off. "I know it doesn't really matter what Lucius looks like. But some of *my* friends have older brothers and sisters in *his* school. And they all know he's my brother. If he goes to that party looking like the . . . *dork* he usually does, it'll get back to my friends, and then *my* reputation will be ruined!"

Misty's doing a good job, I think. She should really be a lawyer like on TV. But does she have to lay it on so thick? I mean, *dork???*

"I see your point," my mom admits.

"Good," Misty says, arms folded across her chest.

"So I'll take Lucius to the stores and help him pick something out just as soon as I'm done here."

"No, Mom." Misty shakes her head vehemently. "That's not going to work."

"What do you mean?" Mom stops folding mid-towel.

Misty gives me and my outfit a lingering once-over, then turns back to Mom. "Do you really think, Mom," she says scathingly, one eyebrow cocked, "that you've been doing such a good job so far?"

I kind of feel sorry for Mom; she looks so wounded.

"Just drive us to the mall." Misty sighs as though she's the oldest person in the world or at least this house. "Then leave us there with the credit card. I'll take care of all the rest."

God, sometimes I wish I had my little sister's self-confidence.

AURORA

Saturday morning comes and I tell my dad I need to get some new clothes.

"What for?" he wants to know.

I can't help it. When I answer I know I sound like a disdainful kid. "For the party Friday night?"

"What's wrong with what you own already?" he says, stating the obvious.

"This is a party," I point out to my dad, "my first *real* party since we moved here."

"Of course," he says, as though a ton of bricks has just fallen on his head. Then he looks really sad and I know what he's thinking: If Mom were alive, she'd have realized the importance of this occasion right away and she'd have been excited to take me shopping for it.

"So where shall we go," he says, forcing a bright smile, "to find the best outfit in the world?"

I don't want to hurt his feelings, but . . .

"Dad," I say gently to soften the blow, "do you think you could just drop me at the mall? Celia and Deanie are going around noon and they asked if I could meet them at the food court."

"Sure thing, princess," my dad says. "No problem."

At the mall, Celia and Deanie and I make quick work of shopping.

Who knew that three girls could shop so quickly?

We sit at a table in the food court, slurping giant Cokes from Sbarro as we review our purchases.

"Those jeans look great on you," I tell Deanie. "I bet Gary will think you look really cool in them."

Deanie has confessed to liking Gary Addams, and she blushes when I say this.

To deflect attention from herself, she turns to Celia.

"I love your new shoes," Deanie says to her. "They make you look so much taller. They make your legs look a mile long. I'll bet Jessup will think you look hot hot hot."

Celia has not confessed to liking Jessup, but we all pretty much know it just the same. And yet I have good reason to think that Jessup doesn't look at her that way, because I've seen him look at me that way. The world, I sometimes think, is filled with someone liking someone who likes someone else who likes someone else.

Who do I like?

"Who did you buy that white blouse for?" Deanie asks me. "Who are you hoping thinks you're hot hot hot?"

Celia looks at me closely, as though she would very much like to know the answer to this too.

But I'm saved, if not by the Devil himself, then by Jessup.

"Ladies." He saunters up to our table. He's alone. "What are you shopping for today?"

"Your party, of course," Deanie says.

Deanie may not always be the sharpest knife in the drawer, and she may sometimes say mean things about other people, but you kind of have to admire her openness. You always know with Deanie exactly what she's thinking, as though there's just a big colander between her brain and her mouth.

"Cool," Jessup says. He's looking at the others, but somehow I feel as though he's talking directly to me when he adds, "I hope you bought something good."

He saunters off, and with a lot of time left before my dad's scheduled to pick me up, I suggest we shop some more.

LUCIUS

We pull up in front of the mall.

Misty hops out, then pokes her hand back through the front passenger's side window and snaps her fingers at Mom, then holds her palm out.

"Card, please," she commands, and we're off.

How did I get this far in life, I wonder, without Misty's help?

Once inside the mall, the skylights running the length of the interior make me feel like we're in a too-bright place.

"So," I say, tempted to shield my eyes and feeling like a mole that has just come out of his hole, blinking against the glare of day. *Where did all these people come from? And why are they all here in one place?*

"Misty!"

"Misty!"

"Misty!"

Oh, God. There are three blondes, and they are running straight toward us.

I do my best to fade into the background, allow Misty a moment with what are obviously her friends.

"You didn't tell us you were coming shopping today!" says Blonde #1.

"Didn't you say you had to study?" says Blonde #2.

"You could have driven here with us!" says Blonde #3.

I wonder what it must be like to be Misty: to have people actually get excited when they see you.

"I did have to study," Misty says, "but then I decided to come shopping with my brother."

Blondes #1, 2, and 3 look around as if hoping to see me.

"Where is he?" Blonde #3 asks. I knew 3 would be trouble.

"Lucius?" Misty calls.

Oh, God. Why did she have to do that?

Still, I can't just run away — I mean, that would look pathetically silly, would it not? — so I slink out from behind my kid sister, give an awkward little hook wave before I even realize what I'm doing.

Oh, God. I gave the hook wave.

Misty identifies Blondes #1, 2, and 3 in order, ignoring my awkwardness and acting as though I am just any old ordinary brother. "This is Kiki, Tiki, and Biki."

Oh, God. Then it's true. There really is a human being named Biki!

And, may I add, she looks like a bitch.

Kiki and Tiki look at me in ways that are friendly enough if a little cautious, while Biki looks at me as though suspecting me of wanting to boil her bunny.

Misty catches Biki's look, and I'm surprised to see she doesn't like it.

"We really have to get going," she says to her three friends, or maybe two friends and an annoyance. "Maybe we'll catch up with you guys later."

"Where do we start looking?" I ask as soon as Kiki, Tiki, and Biki are gone.

"Someplace cool," Misty says as though I am the dimmest brother who ever lived.

"You mean we can't just go to the Nerd Store?" I ask.

"The Nerd Store?" Misty says. Her nose wrinkles in puzzlement. "Where's that?"

"There is no Nerd Store," I say.

She just stares at me vacantly.

I sigh. "It was a joke." Then I smile. "Don't look now, but I think I'm in the process of developing a sense of humor."

"Yeah," Misty deadpans. "Like, any minute now someone's going to offer you your own show on Comedy Central. Come on."

I follow and she leads me to American Eagle Outfitters.

"But I'm not going camping," I say.

"Don't be such a dork all your life," Misty advises.

Just as she's saying this, who should walk out of the store but Jessup Tristan.

Does the whole rest of the world live at the mall?

"Yeah, Hooks," Jessup says to me with a smile, "don't be such a dork all your life." Then he eyes Misty. "Who's this?" he asks me. "Your girlfriend?"

"She's my little sister," I practically bite the words out through gritted teeth.

"Can't say I'm surprised that's all you could get," Jessup says. "But, you know, maybe when she's a little older . . ." He gives her an ugly leering look, tempting me to lunge at him, which I would do except that my parents would lock me away, regardless how good my motivation. Jessup walks away from us. Then he calls over his shoulder, "Happy shopping!"

"Did that guy just call you 'Hooks'?" Misty asks me.

"He did," I say.

"God, what a creep!"

"Tell me about it," I say.

We enter the store and there are so many clothing choices, immediately I feel overwhelmed.

I say as much to Misty and she advises, "Just don't even look at the girls' side of the store and you'll reduce what you're looking at by half. Isn't that better?"

"Not much," I say.

"You're hopeless," Misty says, making straight for racks of guys' shirts.

She picks out a rumpled-looking rugby shirt. It's short-sleeved, bright blue with an alternating darker stripe.

"I don't think so," I say. Then, to make my point, I indicate the sleeves of the shirt I'm wearing. They come down so low on my arms, they even cover the twin flesh-colored lengths of plastic that now pass as my wrists. "I favor the long look."

"Oops, sor-*ry,*" she says, sounding disgruntled as she throws her hands up in the air. "I forgot for a minute: mustn't let the world see what you've got hidden up your sleeves!"

"Right," I say.

"Fine," she says. "Then we'll get something that looks like the style of what you normally wear, but cooler."

She locates a button-down shirt with long sleeves. The shirt is bigger than what I normally wear. The sleeves are wider. And it's black.

"Um, Misty?" I say.

"Hmm?"

"Won't I look like that old dead guy singer Mom and Dad are always listening to if I wear this? You know, what's his name, the only singer who's not blind — Johnny Crash?"

"Johnny *Cash*," she corrects me with an eye roll, which I think is harsh: Am I now to get treated like an idiot for not knowing nerd facts? "And no," she adds with certainty, shoving the shirt at me. "You won't."

Something else catches her eye.

"Ooh!" she says, holding up a pair of jeans. The denim is an almost black blue but very faded in spots. The pants look like they could be twenty years old. "Dark-tinted, crackle-wash, low-rise boot jeans!"

"I can't believe you know all the technical terms for all this stuff," I say. "Are the ankles supposed to be that wide? Are they supposed to look that dirty? *Do people really pay eighty-nine fifty for pants that look like this?*"

Misty thrusts the jeans at me. "Don't be a dork for the rest of your life, Lucius," she says.

I am sensing a refrain here.

"Go try them on," my kid sister commands me, "the shirt too."

I take a few steps, hear the click of tiny footsteps behind me.

"What are you doing?" I say, turning to see Misty standing so close behind me, we practically crash into each other. "You can't follow me into the dressing room."

"No," she says, "but I can wait right outside so you can come out and show me what you look like once you've tried everything on."

I feel like an idiot, trying on clothes with my kid sister waiting right outside the door. *Oh, well,* I tell myself, *at least it's not my mom.* In a way, I have graduated to a higher plane of dorkdom.

But then something happens to me as I try the clothes on. In fact, you could say that this is my Cinderella moment. Even though there is no Fairy Godmother fairy dust, no horses — or was that mice? — turned into footmen, or pumpkins turned into carriages, it still feels exactly like that. Except for the hooks, I look like anybody else. Indeed, as I study myself in the mirror, I think: *Now even* I *would want to hang out with me.*

Still . . .

"Are you sure the pants are supposed to hang this low?" I emerge to show Misty my new look. "I know the tails of my shirt cover it, but I feel as though everyone can see my underwear."

"They're supposed to be that low." Misty rolls her eyes at me. "That's the fashion. And speaking of underwear, you should really do something about yours."

"What?" I feel my cheeks redden. "I am so not going there with you, Misty."

"Well, someone has to tell you. I mean, I've seen your underwear in the laundry basket. You really need to do something about that. Boxers, not briefs — that's where it's at."

"Stop!" I cover my ears with my hooks. "I can't hear you!"

It's while I'm still covering my ears with my hooks that Misty finally takes a good look at me.

She gestures for me to move my hooks away from my ears and I do so with great reluctance, worried that she's about to attack my underwear again.

"Hey!" Her eyes widen as she looks me over. "Not bad, Lucius. Not bad at all."

"Great. Can we go home now?"

But Misty is not done with me yet.

"Okay," Misty says, "now it's time to go get you some boots. And new socks. I've seen those cloth things you put over your feet, the ones with holes in them. Socks aren't supposed to have air conditioning. They're supposed to look like socks, not sock puppets."

"Boots?" I look down at my feet. "What's wrong with my sneakers?"

"I refuse to dignify that with a response," Misty sniffs. "And, anyway, what do you think we got you boot-cut jeans for? So you can wear boots, duh. And I know just where to go to get them. You'll see. They'll be the coolest boots you've ever seen. When you walk, you'll make a distinctive clunking sound and everyone will know it's you."

I have my doubts about whether sounds are the best judge of a boot's worth — and do I really always want other people to hear me coming? — but Misty is so excited about this, it's contagious.

Suddenly I'm feeling downright — dare I say it? — giddy. I know *giddy* is a girl word, but it's how I feel. I, Lucius Wolfe, am going to a party. I, Lucius Wolfe, am the possessor of cool clothes! And I will soon have boots that make a distinctive clunking sound, for better or worse.

I'm still feeling giddy — no wonder girls like shopping so much! — as we exit the store. I'm still feeling giddy as we round the corner and run smack into . . .

Aurora Belle.

I barely note that in her company are Celia and Deanie, standing a pace behind her.

143

"Lucius!" she says.

"Um, Aurora," I say.

"Hey," she says.

"Um, hey," I say.

Okay, I admit it: I'm starting to feel pretty lame right around now.

Aurora looks pointedly at something beside me and I look down at my side and see Misty standing there. Funny how quickly I forgot about her. I look at my sister just long enough to see that she's studying Aurora with the same curious expression with which Aurora is studying her, before shifting my focus back to Aurora, which is exactly where my focus wants to be.

"This is my sister, Misty," I say. Stupidly, I raise the bags in my hooks. "We were just, um, shopping."

"Oh!" Aurora says, looking as relieved as she sounds. "Okay, then! We'd better not keep you." She looks at me a second more, then says, "See ya, Lucius," before walking away.

"See ya, Aurora," I say so quietly, I doubt she or her friends hear me.

I'm watching Aurora walk away, so it's at least a minute before I feel the eyes of Misty boring a hole in the side of my face.

Aurora disappears around a corner and I finally turn to my sister.

"What?" I demand, seeing the look on her face.

"That girl," she says, a light dawning in her eyes, "that *Aurora*. You *like* her."

"Ohhh," I say, feeling disgusted, with myself more than with my sister, "don't be such a dork all your life."

I say this to make her laugh.

I say this to shut her up.

But inside, some of the light has gone out of this day for me. Because I know that no matter how many cool clothes I buy, how many boots that make a distinctive clunking sound when I walk, a girl like Aurora will never like a boy like me.

At least not *in that way*.

AURORA

It's amazing how different jeans look at a party than they do at school.

Everyone here in Jessup's basement has jeans on, like a uniform, as they stand and sit around, listening to loud music while drinking soda and eating chips.

My father, a.k.a. the King of Promptness, dropped me off at seven on the dot. For the first fifteen minutes I was the only one here, but then the place began to fill up.

Not only do people look different somehow, but they act different too. It's like they're more formal, as though we weren't just together a few hours ago. It's like when you go to some function at school at night. Everything is the same — the cast, the setting — but everything is different. And this — not only is it more formal and different, but it's also oddly intimate, being down here in this basement.

"What's new?" Jessup asks me, after offering me another soda.

"Not much," I say. "I'm pretty sure nothing has changed since this afternoon."

"Well, you changed your clothes," he points out. "That top looks nice on you."

"Thanks," I say.

The room is large and fairly dark, with a few old sofas and some beanbag chairs scattered around. There's a wide clearing in the center of it all, as though someone has made room for people to dance — I suspect Jessup's mother's handiwork here — but no one is doing so right now. I think she is probably behind the balloons too, which Steve and Gary are taking great delight in popping. Jessup's yard slopes steeply down from front to back and at the far end of the basement is a set of sliding-glass doors leading out to the back.

I look at the old round clock on the wall — it has roman numerals and a loud ticker — and wonder if everyone who is coming is already here.

LUCIUS

I have my mom drop me off at eight o'clock even though Aurora told me it starts at seven.

I do this because my mom is one of those people who are so punctual, they often arrive places early, like, say, while the hostess is still getting dressed. So I tell my mom the wrong time, since I have no desire to see Mrs. Tristan in her bathrobe and curlers, and I really don't want to be the first one there, with me being the first thing everyone sees upon arrival.

Or maybe I do it because I'm a prima donna and I just want to make my grand entrance . . .

Yeah, right.

Not only is this the first party I've ever gone to without hands, it's the first party I've ever gone to, period.

If I still had palms, they'd be sweating as I wave goodbye to my mom, knock on the Tristans' front door.

A woman I think must be Mrs. Tristan answers. She has hair just like her son's — that freaky brown shading to white gold — and I wonder, forcing down the bubble of hysterical laughter that rises in my throat, if she and Jessup visit the hair stylist together.

"Yes?" She eyes me suspiciously, as though I might be there to rob the place. Another bubble of hysteria threatens as I control the desire to say, *Hey, look, Tristan's ma: no hands!*

"I'm, um, here for your son's party?" I ask-answer.

"Jess-*up!*" Mrs. Tristan bellows as she vacates the doorway and disappears into the house. "Another one of your friends is here!"

Across the hall from the door I'm standing outside of is a second door and I realize it must lead to the basement as it opens and a wall of music follows Jessup to the front door.

"Hooks!" he says, jovially enough, but puzzled too. "What are you doing here?"

"I heard there was a party for all the cast and crew," I say, feeling like an idiot even as I say it. I never should have come.

Jessup digests this for a minute, then says, "Glad you could make it." He holds open the screen door for me while he extends his other hand for a shake.

I just stare at his hand until he pulls it back.

You would think he would be embarrassed, but all he does is smile one of his annoying smiles. "Oops, sorry, Hooks. I forgot there for a second."

I step inside the house, turning to make sure the screen is shut; I have the feeling Mrs. Tristan will hunt me down at home if I let bugs get into her house.

I'm turning back when someone else comes up the stairs.

"Lucius!" Aurora says, and it's obvious she's happy to see me.

I look at Aurora standing there as Jessup stands off to one side. She has on bright blue jeans and a pure white blouse, and the smile she's directing at me is like a thousand-watt bulb turned on in the middle of a dark cave.

What can I say?

I melt.

I melt all over the floor.

149

AURORA

We go back down into the basement, Jessup entering the room first, then me, then Lucius. At home, my dad still has a turntable from his college days on which he sometimes plays old records — real vinyl records! If there's a scratch on one of them, sometimes the needle skips, screeching to the innermost circle of the vinyl as the music halts. Lucius's entrance has that same effect on the room now: like a screechy needle stopping music.

"Do you want something to drink?" I ask Lucius as conversation slowly resumes.

But he just shakes his head. He looks tired, as though it has taken all the energy he has just to get here, just to get to this room. He also looks handsome — or, as Deanie would say, hot hot hot — in his black shirt and boots. Somehow, his jeans look better on him than everyone else's.

"Excuse me," he says formally, as though he has someone he needs to go talk to. But then he just finds one of the vacant beanbag chairs and lowers his body into it. It's like he's on the bus or in the lunchroom: sitting alone, apart.

The music cranks up a notch, soaring louder, and people begin to dance. I figure they all have curfews, just like I do, and they're trying to get in as much as they can as quickly as they can.

Actually, it's just the girls dancing with each other at first. Celia and Deanie are bouncing around like two shiny silver pinballs released into the same machine at the same time. Deanie gestures for me to join them, but I just shake my head. Then Celia grabs hold of Jessup's hand. I can't hear what she's whispering, but I'm sure she's asking him to dance. He shakes his head too. Steve and Gary prove less reluctant to dance with the bouncing pinballs, however, and before long they join Celia and Deanie.

"Are you having fun?" The voice at my side is Jessup's. "It's a good party, right?"

"Yes," I agree, "a good party."

"Then why aren't you dancing?" he asks.

Before I know it, he's grabbing my hand, pulling me out to the middle of the floor. Between the cast and the crew, there must be thirty people dancing here now.

The music is fast, so I don't mind at first — we are just two in a big crowd — but then a slow song comes on, and before I can walk away, Jessup puts his arms around me, pulling me toward him.

Onstage, when we're rehearsing the play, there are scenes that call for Jessup to touch me — some of the dancing scenes and of course the big kissing scene at the end — but his hands on me now feel different from the way they do then.

I feel him pull me close enough so that my breasts are smushed up against his chest. This makes me uncomfortable. There's not a teenage girl in the world who doesn't know that teenage boys are gaga about breasts.

I try to pull away. "I think I need another soda," I say, trying to sound cheerful, peppy.

"C'mon, Sandy," he says, talking to me as though we're running a scene from the play as his arms pull me in tighter still. Then he lowers his head toward mine until there's hardly any space between our lips. "Kiss me," he says.

I turn my face away and insert my arms between our bodies, struggling to break his hold on me, to free myself. If this weren't so annoying, so disturbing, I would laugh: it's like he's the skunk from those old cartoons, Pepe Le Pew, and I'm the French cat, Penelope Pussycat, trying to get away from his amorous embraces. *Le pant, le pew*.

But Jessup is strong.

Over his shoulder, I see Lucius suddenly bolt out of his beanbag chair — a part of my mind marvels: I didn't think it was physically possible to bolt out of a beanbag chair — but before he can get to us, I'm saved by, of all people, Jessup's mother.

"Jessup!" she calls loudly from the foot of the stairs. Mrs. Tristan sounds angry. "I need to speak with you!"

"I'll be back," he says before letting me go and walking away.

I don't watch him go. Instead, my eyes are on Lucius as he retreats back toward his beanbag.

I don't want him to withdraw.

Suddenly I'm tired of being a leaf on the wind. I don't care what Deanie thinks, what Celia thinks, or any of the others for that matter — if I ever did. The others are all wrong about Lucius. All I care about is that he is here now and I don't want him to withdraw.

I place my hand on his upper arm to stop him.

"Dance with me?" I ask.

LUCIUS

Her hand on my arm is soft and strong at the same time.

Truth: I have never danced with a girl before.

Oh, there is so much I have never done with a girl!

The white color of Aurora's shirt makes me suddenly intensely aware of her breasts. What teenage boy, if he prefers girls to boys, is not aware of breasts? You know, the eighth and ninth wonders of the world. And just as suddenly, it occurs to me that I will never get to touch Aurora's breasts or any other girl's breasts, hand against skin, not in the way that other people do.

I have to stop thinking these thoughts.

I feel the eyes of others watching us, like spiders from the corners, but I can't refuse her. Pushing aside my own feelings of embarrassment and awkwardness, I allow Aurora to take hold of my hooks, pulling gently until my arms enclose her, as if I don't know that this is how the dance is supposed to go.

She looks at me closely, then lets her head drop until it is resting lightly against my shoulder.

The room disappears around us.

To hell with breasts right now!

Because I swear I just died and went to heaven.

AURORA

There aren't words to describe how good this feels: Lucius's arms around me. This is where I want to be. And yet I can't escape the feeling of being observed too closely by others, like a bug under glass.

I want to extend this moment and change it, all at the same time. But I can't do that here. Jessup will be back any minute now, and I can't help but think that will change everything.

I go up on tiptoes. I whisper in Lucius's ear:

"Let's go outside."

LUCIUS

The music gradually fades as we go out the sliding-glass doors, shutting everyone and everything behind us, but somehow the silence is better, not just a relief from noise.

The air outside is brisk, and a wan moon hangs halfway up the night sky. There's a wind kicking up, straining the trees in the backyard to one side.

Still, it feels good to be out of doors at night. It occurs to me that many people do this — go outside just for the sake of being outside — and perhaps I should try it sometime at home.

"Nice night," I say, feeling stupid almost immediately — what a stupid thing to say — and yet feeling the need to say something, anything.

"Come on," Aurora says, looking over her shoulder, making sure that I am following as she leads me away from the lights of the house.

AURORA

I just want to kiss him.

Is that so wrong?

I've never kissed any boy before, unless you count kissing Jessup during play rehearsals, which I don't.

When your mom is dying for five years, there's not really a whole lot of time left over in the day for kissing boys.

But now I want to erase those false first kisses with Jessup. A first kiss, I think, should be important, special. It should be with the person you want to kiss more than anybody in the world.

LUCIUS

Her lips — how can I describe them?

Yes, they taste like salt from the chips, sweet from the soda, but I hardly notice that as I drown in the sensation of soft welcome. It is my first kiss and it is like discovering a new country and kissing someone who knows me better than anyone, all at the same time.

After a minute, I pull back. I want to look at her so I can really believe that she is here. With me.

"I thought you might like Jessup," I say, "once upon a time."

"I think you might be nuts," she says, smiles, "once upon a time."

The strong wind whips a stray hair across the front of her face. I long to reach out with a hand, brush that hair out of the way for her, feel that hair, feel that cheek.

More than ever before right now, I wish that I had hands again.

What a glorious thing it would be to hold a girl's hand, *this girl's* hand, to feel her skin beneath my fingers.

I have a wild thought: If I knew her better, I could remove my arm in front of her, ask her to let me rub my stump against her cheek. But this is all still too new, like the creation of a universe. It is a crazy thought, the idea of touching her that way, I know this, but I can't keep the vision from forming in my mind. Perhaps someday.

But that stray hair is still across her face now. Someone needs to do something about it, so I cautiously extend my hook and, using the pincer, gently brush it away for her.

A part of me expects her to recoil at this touch, but she doesn't. Rather, she leans into it, grabbing on to my hook with one of her hands while she rests her cheek against the cold metal.

I cannot escape a simple truth: Against all odds, against all the odds of the universe, against every odd in my life, Aurora likes me.

Previously, I realize, she has always been the one to reach for me. She has always talked first, been friendly first, done everything first. Well, now it is my turn. I dislodge my hook from her hand, place my arms around her, pull her body close to mine. Between the twin layers of our shirts, I can feel her heart beat against my chest. I imagine that in the quiet of the night I can literally *hear* the sound of its pulse.

This moment: it is perfect. I realize that now I am free to like Aurora back, to express that liking. There's just one problem. There's a truth she doesn't know but she should.

I put my lips against her ears, I'm just about to whisper that truth, when we are interrupted.

"God, I can't believe you two!"

It's Jessup.

He turns to glare at me. If more hate could be buried in a look, I've never seen it.

"I'm sorry I ever invited you!" He hurls the words at me before storming back toward the house.

I could almost laugh at this — of course, he *didn't* invite me — but the look he gave me, the look he threw back at Aurora as he stormed away, it is too hate-filled to laugh at. It is dangerous to hate that much.

I know about that kind of hate.

Now I want to save the moment between Aurora and me, bring it back to what it was, but I can see it slipping away into the ugliness of Jessup's outburst.

So what do I do?

I make the moment even worse by choosing to tell Aurora, right then, my truth.

"Remember what I told you about the accident in my basement?"

Her expression is puzzled, like I've begun speaking in a different language, and I realize she's still caught within the spell of Jessup's venom.

"About the day I blew off my hands," I say, speaking almost impatiently. Now that I have decided to tell this, I'm in a hurry to get it out.

I don't wait for her to catch up to me. We can't be . . . *whatever we are* without her knowing the whole truth.

"It was no accident," I say, "not really. I mean, it was an accident that it happened that day, that way. But there was nothing innocent about what I was doing. I was practicing to do harm, somewhere, some time, maybe."

The look on her face: it's as though I've graduated from speaking foreign languages to speaking in tongues as she tries to process the words. I almost wish this moment of her confusion would extend into eternity — if purgatory is in no way heaven, well, at least it is not hell — but then a look of horror overtakes her features.

I can see she gets it now:

I meant to blow up something else and it was only the fickle hand of Fate that prevented me from doing so by taking away my own hands.

I am the monster, the Frankenstein monster that everybody thinks I am.

It's my turn to look on in horror and devastation as Aurora runs away from my story, away from me.

—————

When eleven o'clock comes, I am waiting right outside the front door. I have been standing here for quite some time.

My dad pulls in to the driveway and I climb into the seat beside him.

"So, how was it?" he asks, backing out onto the street, hands at ten and two on the steering wheel as he begins to drive us home. "Was it good?"

"Yes," I say.

I stare out the front windshield. A light rain has started to fall and I watch the wiper blades *swish-swishing* the drops away.

"Yes," I say again. "It was good until it wasn't."

I did not get the chance to tell Aurora, although I wish I had, that I have become grateful to the universe that I blew off my own hands before I could hurt anybody else.

Perhaps it does not matter.

AURORA

I'm so confused.

Could the things that people like Deanie and Celia said about Lucius really be true? Is he crazy?

LUCIUS

On Saturday, on Sunday, I relive the events of Friday night as if it is a slow-motion dream turned into a nightmare that I can't get out of. I remember realizing Aurora liked me, the feel of her lips against mine, the smell of her hair: like rain and cinnamon. I remember seeing the look of horror dawn in her eyes after I told her the truth about myself: she thought I was crazy.

It is like those phantom feelings I get about my hands sometimes, the sensation that I have limbs where I do not. Aurora is like one of those phantoms now. I keep feeling as though she must still be there, and yet I know that she isn't.

Misty has no way of knowing what's happened, although she does ask me about it. I refuse to talk, spending the weekend in a state of monklike silence. It doesn't stop her, however. In an effort to snap me out of my funk, she insists on a marathon session of pool. She even lets me break. It doesn't matter.

I lose every game.

AURORA

Monday morning comes and it's all I can do to drag myself out of bed when the dog alarm goes off; it's all I can do to get myself dressed for school. I don't even bother with brushing my hair one hundred strokes.

"What's wrong?" my dad asked me when he picked me up from Jessup's party.

"What's wrong?" he asks me now as we eat breakfast; or rather, he eats while I just sit.

But I don't tell him, won't tell him, can't tell him:

I was wrong about Lucius.

Lucius is just as crazy as everyone else said he was.

LUCIUS

The day begins terrible and then gets worse.

I wait for Aurora as she gets off the bus, but she won't speak to me.

I want to tell her that it's not quite as awful as it sounds — yes, I wanted to do some damage in the world. Yes, I was angry at life, frustrated, and yes, I knew too much about making explosives, or perhaps not enough, seeing that I blew my own hands off. But no, I had no specific target in mind, just general mayhem and carnage. Maybe I wouldn't have gone through with it. I like to think I wouldn't. Certainly, I would not do the same thing now. I'm a different person now; in part, I think, because of her.

But she won't listen to me.

Nor will she listen to me when I trail her to her locker, try to talk to her there.

"Let it go, Lucius," she says to me, sounding both incredibly tired and sad all at once.

But I can't let it go.

Still, I have no choice as Jessup strolls by and Aurora calls out, "Hey, Jessup! Wait up!"

Her words are like four daggers piercing my armor.

I go out to the nonsmokers' lounge hoping to see Nick Greek.

He is nowhere to be seen.

Early last week he called off our morning football practice sessions, which is why I'm back to taking the bus, and now it occurs to me that I haven't seen him since Thursday. I suppose I was so obsessed with going to that party, I hadn't even thought much about him.

Now I wonder where he is.

I could ask one of the other security guards, but that's really not my way. Plus, whenever Nick is here and talking to me, they always glare at me like I'm a bad influence on him.

I'm just about to give up and go inside when a man enters the area dressed in a dark blue suit. Since most teachers and administrators dress fairly casually, he stands out.

It's Nick; Nick, looking surprisingly handsome, pockmarked cheeks and all.

"I came to say goodbye," he says, without ever having said hello.

"What?" I don't understand.

"I'm on my way to the airport," Nick says, only adding to the mystery, my confusion. "I've got a tryout with an NFL team down in Florida."

Ah. The light in my brain finally clicks on.

"I heard kickers are in high demand this season," he goes on when I fail to speak. "Come to think of it," he adds with a grin, "I think I heard somewhere that kickers are always in demand."

"I think I heard that same thing too," I speak at last.

Nick Greek holds out his hand. It's obvious it's not the unconscious, unthinking gesture others have done. On the contrary, it's very deliberate. He knows exactly what he's doing.

I don't want him to go.

This could not come at a worse time for me. With Aurora gone, no doubt forever, he is the only friend I have left in the world.

But if he is my friend, and he is, then I should want what's best for him.

I reach out my right hook, shake his hand like a man.

"Maybe this year I'll be great," Nick says. "Maybe next year I'll be a goat. But I gotta try."

"You'll be great every year," I say.

"Well, then . . ."

There's nothing left to say.

Nick starts to walk away, then stops, calls over his shoulder: "Thanks, Lucius. If it wasn't for you . . ."

Before he can say anything further, I salute him with my hook. I let him go.

AURORA

A day that begins terrible and then gets worse turns into the worst day of my life.

It's Deanie who tells me what's happened, not long after third period. I stand outside the door to our American History classroom and listen, not believing the words I'm hearing. Then I look at her face to see if she's telling the truth or if this is some kind of sick joke.

Immediately I can tell it is the truth. What I can't tell, looking in her eyes, is if she's glad to be the bearer of bad tidings or not.

Lucius is not only crazy. He's evil.

LUCIUS

I'm standing in front of my own locker when I feel the tap, hard, on my shoulder. I'm standing in front of my locker not because I need to put anything in it or get anything from it but rather because I have no idea where I should be anymore.

I turn around and see Aurora standing there.

I'm so happy to see her. She must have forgiven me, or at the very least, she must be willing to talk to me some more about it. Maybe she just wants to try to understand. That would be like her.

I open my mouth to speak. I want to tell her how relieved I am that she wants to talk to me.

That's when she reaches out with an open palm and slaps me hard across the face.

"You are . . ." She is so angry, she has no word to describe what I am, leaving vacant space to describe me instead.

My face is still stinging from the slap, but I couldn't care less about that.

"I just can't believe it," she says. "I can't believe you would be so hateful."

I have done more than one hateful thing in my life; I know this, and I am trying to get better.

But in this moment, I have no clue as to what she's talking about.

AURORA

I don't care what Deanie said. I don't care what everyone is saying now about my father. They're wrong, wrong, *wrong*.

I'm not there to witness it, but others are all too eager to tell me what happened.

"They took your dad away for questioning," Deanie says.

"They didn't have cuffs on him or anything," Celia says. "I think they just want to talk to him. My dad says he's been suspended . . . indefinitely."

I remember, in some dim corner of my brain, that Celia's father, Mr. Wentworth, is the vice principal here.

"I'm sorry," Jessup says, and I can tell he means it.

I'm sorry too.

LUCIUS

I have no idea what's happened.

One talent I have acquired since the explosion is the ability to just be quiet and listen and watch. So as the day goes on, I learn enough to realize that whatever has happened, it has something to do with Mr. Belle, Aurora's father.

I watch Jessup with Aurora at lunch. Something has changed between them. Whereas before I could see that he relentlessly pursued her while she resisted, now it is as though she is leaning on him. When she doesn't eat any of her lunch, Jessup goes up to the cafeteria line and waits patiently — it is a very long line — to get a carton of chocolate milk to try to tempt her. When Celia sits down in the place Jessup has vacated — meaning that now Aurora is flanked by Celia and Deanie, leaving no place beside Aurora for Jessup when he returns, so he will have to sit on the other side of Celia — Jessup tells her to move. He makes his request politely, but it's obvious that it is more of a command. The look on Celia's face? It's clear to me at least that she expected something different from him. I am puzzled: Did she really think that for some insane reason Jessup would stop liking Aurora and would turn his attentions to her instead? Why would he? I am sure Celia has her share of attractions, for some — most people do, with the possible exception of me — but why would any guy turn from the possibility of Aurora to that of any other girl?

Aurora, still not eating, excuses herself from the others. I watch as she goes over to the cafeteria monitor and I assume she asks for a pass to go to the library or study hall. Well, perhaps not the library. It would probably be too sad for her there now without Mr. Belle.

Her shoulders are slumped as she exits the cafeteria. She looks so sad. And even though she slapped me, even though she has turned her back on me, this impresses me as *wrong*. Yes, there are plenty enough bad things that go on in this life — enough sadness in the world to make a person cry if he thought about it too much, or to make him want to blow up something — but it is not right that Aurora should feel so sad. It makes me want to fix it for her.

People may say, as they have often, that there is something broken in me. But I want to fix what's broken in her.

It's only after the door closes behind Aurora that I start paying attention to the conversation at Jessup's table again. It's only after she's safely gone that I hear Jessup say to the others in a smirking tone of voice:

"I always knew that librarian was crazy."

Then he drinks the rest of Aurora's chocolate milk, crushes the empty carton within his fist, and tosses it in the direction of the garbage pail.

It is with some satisfaction I note that he misses, and by a rather wide margin.

Still, I cannot believe what I have just heard.

I know crazy and — believe it or not — I do know normal. And I've met Mr. Belle, spoken to him in his home.

Mr. Belle isn't crazy.

Mr. Belle is the most normal human being I've ever met.

AURORA

I want to skip play rehearsal after school. I want to go home to be with my dad. But the school secretary gives me a message from him. The message says that he's all right, but that he's very busy and he wants me to stay for rehearsal, take the late bus home.

So it appears, whether I want it to or not, the show must go on.

LUCIUS

I go to rehearsal where, I learn, I have become a pariah.

What's worse, I wonder, to be a pariah or a piranha?

Easy answer: a piranha.

It's true that at Jessup's party, no one other than Aurora was exactly what you could call friendly to me. But the last few weeks we've been rehearsing, I've seen a respect for me grow in the eyes of the cast and crew. Again, if not friendly, they've clearly recognized that I am the go-to person in this production and they have all been going to me for help.

But now no one asks me for anything, no one listens to me when I speak. I might as well not even be here.

What is going on now reminds me of a story my dad used to like to tell back before the explosion, when he was still what he and my mom referred to as an HG: Happy Guy.

My mom and dad used to have this agreed upon theory that you could divide everyone in the entire world into just two types: HG, for Happy Guy, and MG, for Miserable Guy, and that these tags applied to females too, because no matter what the gender, all human beings were either Happy Guys or Miserable Guys. My mom and dad claimed you could determine who was which at a glance, but that it was easiest to do with celebrities or politicians, people that others already had an opinion about. It had to do with their basic nature, though, not their general fortune or lack thereof. Jon Stewart? Happy Guy. Tom Cruise? Miserable Guy. George Bush? Miserable Guy. Bill Clinton? Happy Guy.

"Bill Clinton," my dad used to observe. "You could tell just from looking at him, that even when times were at their worst, he was still having a blast every day of his life."

Aurora Belle? Happy Guy.

Lucius Wolfe? Well, on him, the jury is still out. He used to be a Miserable Guy, just like his dad used to be a Happy Guy. And maybe, one day, his dad will be again. According to my parents, it's possible under extraordinary circumstances for a person to make the leap from Happy Guy to Miserable Guy and vice versa.

So you see, before this all happened to my family, before the explosion, both my parents were Happy Guys, and Misty too. I was the only MG in our old household. So you see, too, I don't blame my parents for what I became and never have. It wasn't my parents' fault I wanted to blow something up. It wasn't my parents' fault I was so angry with the world. And why was I so angry? I suppose — and I know this is no excuse, but it is the reason — I was exhausted with being so different from everybody else. Intelligence can be an isolating thing, and I grew lonely. And it does get weary-making, not to mention anger-making, always being the guy who gets shoved into his own locker, gets called Hooks.

Sure, many, many people survive extended abuse or bullying and never snap. But some do snap. It is a thing, I think, worth thinking about.

So much of life can be divided into before and after. It's as though whenever there is a significant event, there's a picture with two sides that look remarkably similar, but not quite, and right down the center is an invisible line representing that event. This is Lucius *before*. This is Lucius *after*. This is the Wolfe family *before*. This is the Wolfe family *after*. Two slightly different versions of the same picture, the second image like a smoky mirror. It kind of makes you wonder what *after* would look like were it not for the existence of that line.

But anyway, getting back to the story my dad used to like to tell, back before the explosion, before he became an MG.

My dad said there was this man in Japan who worked for a company. The company wanted to get rid of the man because he was getting old; I'm not sure if it was because he was no longer doing his job properly or if they just didn't want to pay his salary anymore. But they didn't want to be rude and fire him. So what did they do instead? First, they kept moving him to increasingly smaller offices, I suppose in the hopes that he would just quit. When that didn't work, they moved him to an office in the basement. They also stopped giving him any work to do, so he had nothing to do there all day long, alone. Finally, when nothing else worked, they began dimming the electricity in his basement office each day so that the lights over his empty desk grew gradually less illuminating until one day there was no light left. When he was in complete darkness, they got their way and he resigned.

I have no idea what is going on, what is happening to me. All I know is that I am like that little Japanese man sitting in the basement: alone, as all around me the lights slowly go out.

But I'm not going to quit.

I will not quit.

AURORA

I get off the late bus, run to the house, tear open the door, and find my father at the kitchen table.

He's just sitting there, head in his hands.

"Daddy?" I say.

He looks up, sees me looking at him. I swear, those are tears in his eyes.

"I didn't do it, princess," he says. "Whatever they're saying, I didn't do it."

I feel a knot of sadness in the pit of my stomach that grows, threatening to overwhelm me, sadness that he could even think for a second that I would believe anything bad about him.

"Of course not!" I cry. I move to sit at the table, take one of his large hands in mine. "But what happened?"

"One of the students . . ." He pauses. "One of the *female* students . . . leveled an accusation of improper conduct at me."

"I know," I say.

"She said I made . . . *inappropriate advances.*"

"I know that too, Daddy." I don't want to say the next, I don't want to hurt him any more than he's already been hurt, but surely he must already know. "Everyone at school is talking about it."

He releases a heavy sigh. "Yes," he says, "I suspect they are."

"Who is she, Daddy?" I need to know. "Who is saying these awful things?"

"I'm not at liberty to say," he says.

"'Not at . . .'"

I can't believe he won't tell me!

I think back how, after the party Friday night, when he picked me up, he wanted to know what was wrong. And I refused to tell him. Now he is refusing to tell me something crucial. But this is different.

"You have to tell me," I say. "I can find a way to fix this!"

"No," he says. "She's a minor. I've been ordered not to discuss the specifics while the investigation is pending."

I feel so helpless.

"But I can tell you this: Mr. Wentworth says that it's not just a matter of her word against mine. There's another student, a boy, who can corroborate everything the girl has said."

Yes. I'd heard that too.

It was why I struck Lucius.

Deanie told me that Celia told her that she heard from her father — the vice principal, Mr. Wentworth — that Lucius was the one who corroborated the story about my father, saying he saw the incident. But Deanie claimed Celia said that Mr. Wentworth wouldn't tell her the girl's name because they needed to protect her.

In my mind, I can still hear the sound of my hand striking against Lucius's cheek, still feel the backlash sting of his cheek against my open palm.

If he were here in front of me right now, I would hit him again.

I can't believe we ever invited him into our home.

I can't believe he could be so vengeful.

He told me he once wanted to blow something up, and now he has blown up my world.

Everything everybody said about him is true.

LUCIUS

Two more weeks pass and almost nothing changes.

Mr. Belle's suspension continues — pending further investigation — and now I know what he is being investigated for: trying something improper with one of the female students.

How could any sane person believe such a thing of him?

I know this can't be true.

I wish that I could prove it.

Also in the Nothing Changes column: the way other people treat me. I am still pariah non grata at rehearsals, but I am no elderly Japanese businessman toiling away in the basement of Heartless Employer Inc. and I refuse to quit. Let the other cast and crew petition for my removal if they want me gone so badly.

One thing that does change, and I confess this upsets me deeply: I see Aurora growing even closer to Jessup. Their scenes together as we edge toward opening night on Friday take on a real-life quality that goes beyond mere acting. It makes my stomach churn, and yet on some level higher than my usual self, I'm grateful that she has someone to lean on, even if that someone isn't me.

Still, I worry about Aurora, worry about Mr. Belle. So on Thursday, rather than sticking around for the final rehearsal, I tell Mrs. Peepers I'm not feeling well and take the regular bus instead of the late one. Her expression tells me that even though we are just one day away from opening night, she's picked up on the coolness of the cast and crew toward me and she knows my presence won't be missed.

Once on the bus, rather than getting off at my own stop, I get off at Aurora's. As I knock on the door with my hook, I worry that Aurora might have told Mr. Belle what I told her about myself the night of Jessup's party and I pray that he won't turn me away.

"Lucius." There's no surprise in his tone at seeing me, his delivery is so flat, which is in itself surprising. But when I look into his eyes I see that his usual cheerful light has gone out. His face looks haggard. His hair, what little he has, is untidy, and he's not even wearing a tie. Mr. Belle always wears a tie, to the point where it's easy to picture a newborn baby Mr. Belle, diaper sagging but tie perfectly tied around his wrinkled baby neck. I know what crazy looks like and what normal looks like. I also know what depression looks like. It looks like this.

"Aurora's not here," he says.

"I know that, sir," I say. "Can I come in?"

He looks like he'd like to refuse but then can't think of a good reason why, so he holds open the door for me.

"Please," he says.

"Can I get you something to drink?" he offers once I'm inside, forcing a pasted smile on his face. It's as though someone turned on a switch in him: This is the way to act when company comes calling.

"No, thank you, sir," I say. "I came because I want to help Aurora. I want to help you."

"How can you help?"

"If you would just tell me what happened. If you would just tell me who is spreading these terrible rumors about you —"

"I can't tell you that, Lucius."

"Can't? Or won't?"

"Can't. It's not just a matter of protecting the identity of a minor." He pauses. "It's a matter of *who* that minor is."

Mr. Belle doesn't realize it, but he's just provided me with a valuable bit of information, something I didn't know before.

I've said it before and I'll say it again: If a person sits back and just watches, listens, rather than participating in all the noise around, it is amazing what a person will see and hear, what even a socially challenged person like me can piece together about what is really going on in any given scene.

"You don't have to tell me anything else, sir. I'll take care of this for you, for Aurora."

I can tell he has no idea what I'm talking about, and yet he looks suddenly relieved, as though a great burden has been lifted.

"Why would you help us?" he still wants to know.

I can't believe I'm saying this out loud even as I speak the words, "Because I'm Aurora's Gallowglass." I pause. "Do you know what a Gallowglass is, sir?"

A smile breaks across Mr. Belle's face and I think it must be the first smile he has allowed himself in a very long time.

"Why, yes, Lucius," he says. "Yes, I do."

AURORA

I look in the mirror, start to put my makeup on.

We're all backstage, getting ready for the show.

A part of me is excited about performing — we've been working so long and hard for this moment — but I wish my dad could be here. He's been forbidden to set foot on school grounds, so Mr. Wentworth, Celia's father, drove me here with them. I tried to talk to Mr. Wentworth about it — how could he believe my dad would ever do anything so wrong? — but he said that under the circumstances he couldn't discuss it with me. All the while, Celia stared out the window, as though not wanting to hear what we were saying.

Jessup passes behind me now, stops to place a hand on my shoulder.

"You're going to be great," he says. "Knock 'em dead."

I'm still not sure how I feel about Jessup. I don't really feel as though I *like him* like him, but I am grateful for how kind he's been to me since all this trouble started with my dad. I suppose there are worse reasons for being with a guy. And maybe if I go on being with him, I'll learn to like him the way he wants me to.

I look around the backstage area, relieved that the stage manager is nowhere in sight.

LUCIUS

I wait through all of Act One and half of Act Two before making my move.

Jessup-as-Danny and the other guys are onstage singing "Alone at the Drive-In Movie," Aurora has gone to change because her next time on stage is still three scenes away, and I corner Celia coming out of the girls' room.

"Out of my way, Hooks," she says dismissively.

"No," I say. I take my hooks, plant each one firmly on the walls beside her, effectively cornering her. "I don't think so."

"What are you doing?" she demands. She looks at me wildly, as though she expects me to try to kiss her.

As if.

Hey, look at me: I'm learning to talk like other kids.

"How did it all start?" I ask her. "Was it your idea, or did someone else put you up to it?"

"I don't know what you're talking about," she says, but her eyes say her mouth is lying. Her eyes say, *How does he know???*

"Of course you do," I say. "And you're going to tell me all about it, right now, or I'll go right out onto that stage and announce to the whole school what you did."

It is amazing how cowardly cowards can be.

Celia caves in the face of a greater force: me.

"It was all Jessup's idea," she says. "He made me do it. He said that Mr. Belle was a creep anyway."

Jessup was mad the night he caught Aurora with me, and this has been his revenge. He hurt her greatly, and somehow — I'm not sure quite how he did this yet — destroyed my chances with her while at the same time granting himself the opportunity to pick up the pieces. It's too bad I despise him so much in this moment, because if I didn't, I would want to play chess with him. Of course, I would beat him.

"And why did you do it?" I ask.

"Because I like Jessup and" — her lip quivers here — "I thought that if I did what he wanted, he'd finally like me back."

"But it didn't work out that way, did it?" I point out. I could almost feel sorry for her, pathetic person that she is, were it not for the harm she's caused to Aurora and Mr. Belle. It's awful to plot destruction only to have it all blow up in your face. Of course, having it blow up in your own face is no doubt preferable to causing external destruction.

"No," she says, "but by then it was too late. I'd already told my dad and he believed me."

"But it was just your word against Mr. Belle's."

"But my dad is the vice principal." She pauses. "And Jessup went with me, told them he saw what happened, that he came into the library but that Mr. Belle didn't see him there."

I can tell there's something she's not telling me. A master at leaving crucial bits of information out, I know when someone else is doing it to me.

"What else?" I say.

"And . . . and . . . and we spread the rumor throughout the school that you were the one who said you saw Mr. Belle trying to do something with one of the female students. Jessup may have been the one who told my dad he saw what happened, but then Jessup told me to tell Deanie it was really you. And Deanie, being Deanie, of course she went straight to Aurora and then everyone else in the play. So they got a different story than the one my dad got. They all think you helped destroy Aurora's father."

So that's why Aurora struck me on the face that day, that's why she turned away from me.

I can't say that I blame her.

"Okay, here's what you're going to do," I tell Celia. "You're going to finish the play as if nothing's happened."

"As if nothing's happened? But I can't —"

"*And* you won't breathe a word of our little talk to Jessup, not until *after* the play. I'll know if you do and if you do, I'll go right out on that stage and —"

"Okay, Lucius. I'll do it the way you want."

<hr>

Five minutes later, Celia-as-Rizzo is onstage singing "There Are Worse Things I Could Do" — ironic title, since from where I'm looking at things, there really aren't — when I take my stroll into the audience to locate Mr. Wentworth in the front row.

I squat down beside his seat, whisper a story in his ear, a tale of love and betrayal.

At first, I can tell he doesn't believe me.

"Ask her yourself, sir," I say, "right after the show, her and Jessup too. She'll tell you." I almost pity him as I add, "Kids are capable of doing terrible things."

Then I tell him to call Mr. Belle at home. If Mr. Belle hurries, he can make it to the auditorium just in time to see his daughter close the show.

———•———

I stand in the wings watching the final song: "We Go Together." It's a silly song, but I have learned to enjoy the catchy beat.

Peering out into the audience, I see my parents and Misty in the middle of the auditorium, and I think I catch a glimpse of Mr. Belle standing behind the back row, tie perfectly in place. But maybe I just see it because I want to see it.

I turn my eyes back to the action on the stage.

I've made sure that no one has said anything yet, because I don't want to spoil this night for Aurora.

And even though it galls me to watch Jessup kiss Aurora one last time as the curtain comes down, I allow her this moment of acting triumph onstage, this last moment of innocence *before* what must surely come *after*.

AURORA

I see my dad. I can't believe he's here! But how . . .

My dad gives me a bouquet of roses and a long hug before letting me go.

"How did —" I start to say.

But my dad simply smiles, juts his chin toward the wings of the stage where waits Lucius.

Lucius?

My dad is trying to tell me that Lucius has achieved this miracle? *Lucius?* But how?

I don't see the details, not yet, but I do see that it is true. And I also see quite clearly what Lucius has always been.

Back when my mom was sick all those years, whenever she'd have chemotherapy and in the awful days following, I'd read to her from the encyclopedia to take her mind off the pain. It was always the encyclopedia, because she was obsessed with learning everything there was to know in the world before she died.

We only made it up to G.

But under G, fairly early on, there was an entry for *Gallowglass.*

Centuries ago, Gallowglass were elite foreign military soldiers. Really, a person couldn't do better than to have a Gallowglass for a bodyguard, because they would suffer greatly themselves to protect those they served, they would die if need be while upholding honor.

Lucius may be a flawed human being — as am I, as are we

all — but he is my Gallowglass. He has been since the moment I first saw him.

In the instant I realize this, I see Lucius turn away, his back to the stage; and in the next, I see Jessup run out from the wings on the other side, stopping only long enough to snatch up a prop from the play.

It is a tire iron, the one used during the scene where the Burger Palace Boys pretend to do work on the T-Bird that forms the centerpiece of the set: Greased Lightning.

LUCIUS

I hear the threat, the sound of footsteps pounding with only a slight pause in their progress across the stage, before I see the source. Since everyone else has disappeared from the wings, those angrily rushing footsteps can only be coming for one person: me.

The plastic arm of my prosthetic becomes the perfect blocking device as I whirl to face my attacker, my shoulder recoiling as it absorbs the percussive force of the tire iron.

"You sonofabitch!" Jessup shouts at me, swinging the tire iron at my other side.

"Actually," I say, deflecting the tire iron with the plastic arm of my other prosthetic, "my mother is a fine woman."

I don't even mean it to be funny. But if I am to die tonight, I will not have this cretin defaming my mother before fate and circumstance turn out the lights on my life. My mother is a fine woman, who has only been hurt by me. Really, most of the people in my world are fine people, also hurt by me.

Jessup is swinging wildly at me now.

"This is all your fault!" he says. "If it weren't for you —"

"If it weren't for me *what?*" I continue to deflect each blow, no matter how quickly they come. "If it weren't for me, you would be a better person than you are?" Really, I am so good at deflecting, I think maybe I should give up pool and take up martial arts. "If it weren't for me, you wouldn't do terrible things?"

Jessup lunges at my stomach with the tire iron and I leap backwards.

"We are all responsible for what we do," I tell him. "If I didn't exist, you would still be you."

This time he comes down straight toward my head, and this time when I deflect, I do so with such force, it knocks the tire iron loose from his grip.

He looks so vulnerable without his useless weapon.

In that instant, I hate him for all the unnecessary harm he put Aurora through. I could kill him for that, even make a menacing step in that direction. But in the next instant, I take in the sound of Aurora's voice. She's yelling something, yet all I can make out is the sound of my own name. And when I look over, I see her straining toward me. She is struggling to get free from the arms of Mr. Belle, who is holding her tight from behind. I don't blame him for this. It is exactly what I would do: protect Aurora from any and all harm.

The fight leaves me then.

I no longer want to kill Jessup.

I no longer want to be a monster.

Bending, I pick up the tire iron with my hook, offer it to Jessup. I am thinking I should have died in that explosion. I am thinking, if he wants to kill me, this is a fine enough night to die. I would rather be killed than to kill.

"Go on," I say.

But apparently the fight has gone out of Jessup too, because all he does is stare at the tire iron in my hook, horrified at the sight of it.

"Come on, Jessup," I hear the voice of Mr. Belle, speaking with more gentleness, grace, and forgiveness than I would be able to muster were I him. "You need to get some help."

Then they're gone. Everyone, save one person, is gone.

In this light, my Dark Angel looks amazing.

In any light, really.

AURORA

I kiss the boy.

LUCIUS

I kiss the girl.